EARLIER AMERICAN MUSIC
EDITED BY H. WILEY HITCHCOCK
for the *Music Library Association*

10

THE DAWNING OF MUSIC IN KENTUCKY

THE WESTERN MINSTREL

ANTHONY PHILIP HEINRICH

THE DAWNING OF MUSIC IN KENTUCKY

Or the Pleasures of Harmony in the Solitudes of Nature

(Opera Prima)

THE WESTERN MINSTREL

(Opera Seconda)

INTRODUCTION BY H. WILEY HITCHCOCK
Director, Institute for Studies in American Music,
Brooklyn College, CUNY

DA CAPO PRESS • NEW YORK • 1972

This Da Capo Press edition of *The Dawning of Music in Kentucky* and *The Western Minstrel* is an unabridged republication of the 1820 edition published in Philadelphia.

The consecutive pagination of the original edition, which is followed in this reprint, is confusing and contains a number of errors. In *The Dawning of Music in Kentucky,* page numbers 148-149, 218, and 252-253 are missing from the sequence; an unpaginated leaf appears between pages 96 and 97; and page 187 is blank. In *The Western Minstrel,* page numbers 8-10, 18-21, and 28-31 are missing.

Library of Congress Catalog Card Number 79-39732
ISBN 0-306-77310-4

Published by Da Capo Press, Inc.
A Subsidiary of Plenum Publishing Corporation
227 West 17th Street, New York, New York 10011

Manufactured in the United States of America

EDITOR'S FOREWORD

American musical culture, from Colonial and Federal Era days on, has been reflected in an astonishing production of printed music of all kinds: by 1820, for instance, more than fifteen thousand musical publications had issued from American presses. Fads, fashions, and tastes have changed so rapidly in our history, however, that comparatively little earlier American music has remained in print. On the other hand, the past few decades have seen an explosion of interest in earlier American culture, including earlier American music. College and university courses in American civilization and American music have proliferated; recording companies have found a surprising response to earlier American composers and their music; a wave of interest in folk and popular music of past eras has opened up byways of musical experience unimagined only a short time ago.

It seems an opportune moment, therefore, to make available for study and enjoyment—and as an aid to furthering performance of earlier American music—works of significance that exist today only in a few scattered copies of publications long out of print, and works that may be well known only in later editions or arrangements having little relationship to the original compositions.

Earlier American Music is planned around several types of musical scores to be reprinted from early editions of the eighteenth, nineteenth, and early twentieth centuries. The categories are as follows:

Songs and other solo vocal music
Choral music and part-songs
Solo keyboard music
Chamber music
Orchestral music and concertos
Dance music and marches for band
Theater music

The idea of *Earlier American Music* originated in a paper read before the Music Library Association in February, 1968, and published under the title "A Monumenta Americana?" in the Association's journal, *Notes* (September, 1968). It seems most appropriate, therefore, for the Music Library Association to sponsor this series. We hope *Earlier American Music* will stimulate further study and performance of musical Americana.

H. Wiley Hitchcock

INTRODUCTION

Anthony Philip Heinrich was born in Bohemia in 1781, emigrated to America about 1810, and died in New York in 1861. He was this country's first — and unquestionably most enthusiastic — Romantic nationalist in music. Intoxicated with the natural grandeur of the New World, fascinated with the history of his adopted revolutionary country, enchanted with the American Indian as "noble savage," and above all eager to be called an "American Musician," he poured out hundreds of pieces of the most extravagantly bizarre Romantic programmatism. Most of these were on American subjects, although his musical speech remained essentially that of central Europe.

The Dawning of Music in Kentucky certainly must be the most extraordinary Opus 1 in the history of music. Heinrich was touching forty when he published it. By his own admission he had never composed earlier; to a pathetic plea for funds written late in his life (1856), he was to add this postscript:

> P.S. The Composer did not commence writing music until verging upon the fortieth year of his age, when dwelling by chance in the then solitary wilds and primeval forests of Kentucky. It was from a mere accident that music ever became his profession. . . .

But what an explosion of notes then! Heinrich himself summarized the contents of his "Opera Prima" as including "*Songs* and *Airs* for the *Voice* and *Pianoforte, Waltzes, Cotillions, Minuets, Polonaises, Marches, Variations* with some pieces of a national character adapted for the Piano Forte and also calculated for the lovers of the Violin." He might also have noted that he included a minuet version of *Hail! Columbia* (pp. 71–73) and a waltz version of *Yankee Doodle* (74–76); that the "military waltz," *Avance et Retraite* (115–19), is to live up to its title by being played from beginning to end, then backwards to the beginning again; that *A Chromatic Ramble, of the Peregrine Harmonist* (135–45) is a tour de force of enharmonic complexity (this is one piece that literally must be seen to be believed); and that the collection is crowned with a fantastic quintet for piano and strings, *The Yankee Doodleiad* (252–69), based on trumpet calls, *Hail! Columbia,* and *Yankee Doodle* (with fourteen variations, interrupted in the middle by an interlude on *The President's March* labeled "Huzza for Washington!").

In sum, both *The Dawning of Music in Kentucky* and its slighter companion volume, *The Western Minstrel,* quite completely bear out their composer's characterization of his music as "full of strange ideal somersets and capriccios."

H.W.H.

THE DAWNING OF MUSIC IN KENTUCKY

THE Dawning OF Music IN KENTUCKY, OR THE Pleasures OF Harmony IN THE Solitudes of Nature.

OPERA PRIMA.

BY

A. P. Heinrich.

Pub.d by Bacon & Hart Phila.a

and by the AUTHOR Kentucky.

In presenting this work to the world, the Author observes, that he has been actuated much less by any pecuniary interest, than zeal, in furnishing a Volume of various Musical Compositions, which, it is hoped, will prove both useful and entertaining.

The many and severe animadversions, so long and repeatedly cast on the talent for Music in this Country, has been one of the chief motives of the Author, in the exercise of his abilities; and should he be able, by this effort, to create but one single Star in the West, no one would ever be more proud than himself, to be called an American Musician.— He however is fully aware of the dangers which, at the present day, attend talent on the crowded and difficult road of eminence; but fears of just criticism, by Competent Masters, should never retard the enthusiasm of genius, when ambitious of producing works more lasting than the too many Butterfly-effusions of the present age.— He, therefore, relying on the candour of the Public, will rest confident, that justice will be done, by due comparisons with the works of other Authors (celebrated for their merit, especially as regards Instrumental execution) but who have never, like him, been thrown, as it were, by discordant events, far from the emporiums of musical science, into the isolated wilds of nature, where he invoked his Muse, tutored only by Alma Mater.

A. P. Heinrich,

Kentucky.

 Pr:62.

Philadelphia Published by BACON & HART and by the AUTHOR Kentucky.

Brillante.
O! smile = = = not ye fair = = = = if ye smile = = =
= = not to praise = = = = = = The first = = = = = lings of gen = = =
= = ius a = far = = = = = in the West = = = = Where the dawn = = = ing of
mu = = = sic so faint = = = = ly dis = plays = = = = The sun = = =

= = beams of sci = = = ence to wel = = = = = = = = = = = come its
sf
14
best.
For tho' it be twilight,
sostenuto.
thy smiles could dif=fuse The bright=ness of day on

each ef=fort of Art = = = = = = = = = = = = = = = And in=

ad lib= a tempo.

= spire = = = = = = the Vo = = = t'ry of Sol = = = = i = tude's

Muse = = = = = = To chal = = = = lenge the judg = = = = = = = = =

= ment and = = = = = rav = ish the heart

ff

sf

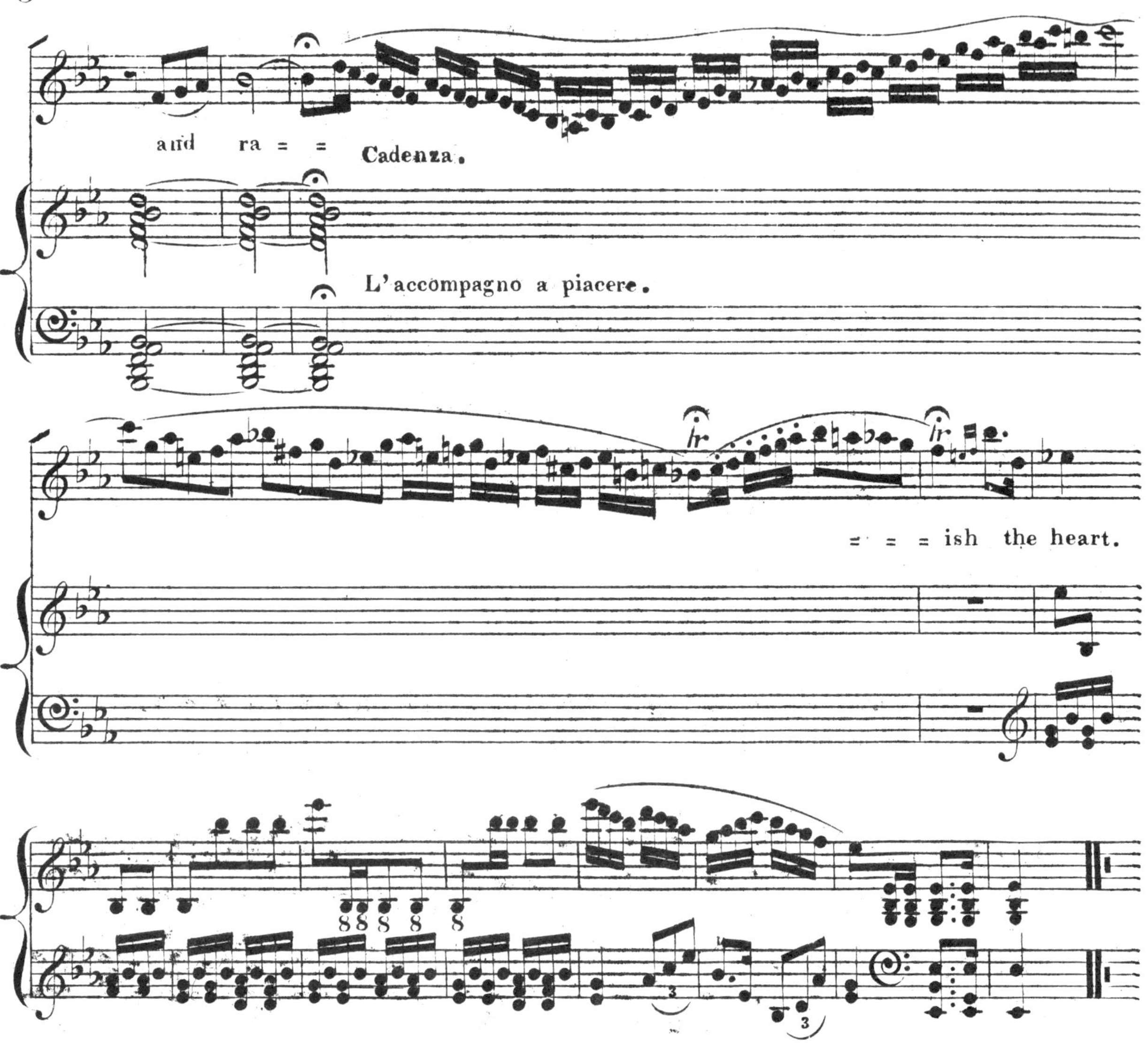

2

But the warmest of wishes the Bard has possest,
Next to that which desires the kindness of eyes,
Is to blot the aspersion so often exprest,
That no music descends from American skies!
Where all that is beautiful, grand, and sublime —
The forest, the meadow, the prairie, and waste,
The mountains of wonder, and waters of time,
Unite to inspire true genius and taste!

3

Tho tutor'd by Nature — self taught in her schools
He has not despis'd the true principles known,
But when Fancy directed, unfetter'd by rules,
He soar'd to those realms which that fancy had shown!

And if he has fail'd,(in those freedoms,) to please,
He humbly begs pardon of all they offend;
But if they give pleasure, with natural ease,
He hopes then to merit the praise of each friend.

4

Then go to the world, from thy solitude go,
Thou beguiler of many and many an hour!
And fear not the frowns of the prejudic'd brow,
Tho young from the land of the oak and the flow'r!
Yes! go and fear not! for thy Lovers are true,
The Sons and the Daughters of Harmony blest!
And should a fair laurel but blossom in view,
How bright it would gleam, like a Star in the West!

TO THE AIR OF "HAIL TO KENTUCKY."

fuse; The brightness of day on each ef = fort of art, And in = spire the vot'ry of sol = i =

ad lib = a tempo.

= tude's muse, To challenge the judgment and rav = = = = ish the heart.

c. L. c. L.

note di scelta.

Canto Da Capo.

Hail to Kentucky

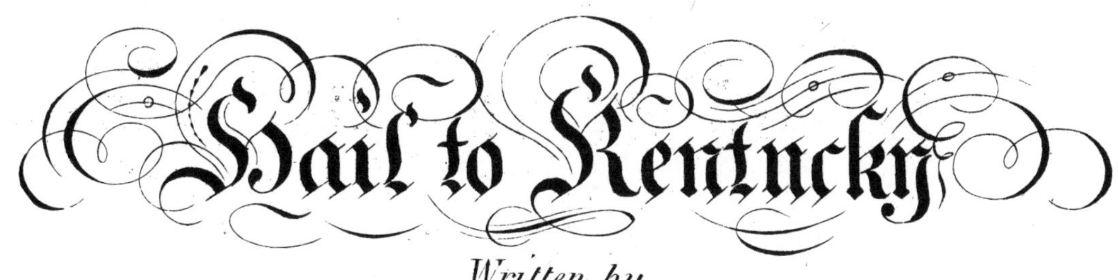

Written by

P. GRAYSON ESQ^R.

(Bardstown Ky.) Composed by

A. P. Heinrich.

The following Music is composed for Orchestra effect, and if found too difficult for Tyro Performers, Professors can with little trouble render it suitable to any capacity —

 Pr. 75.

Philadelphia, Published by BACON & HART, and by the AUTHOR, Kentucky.

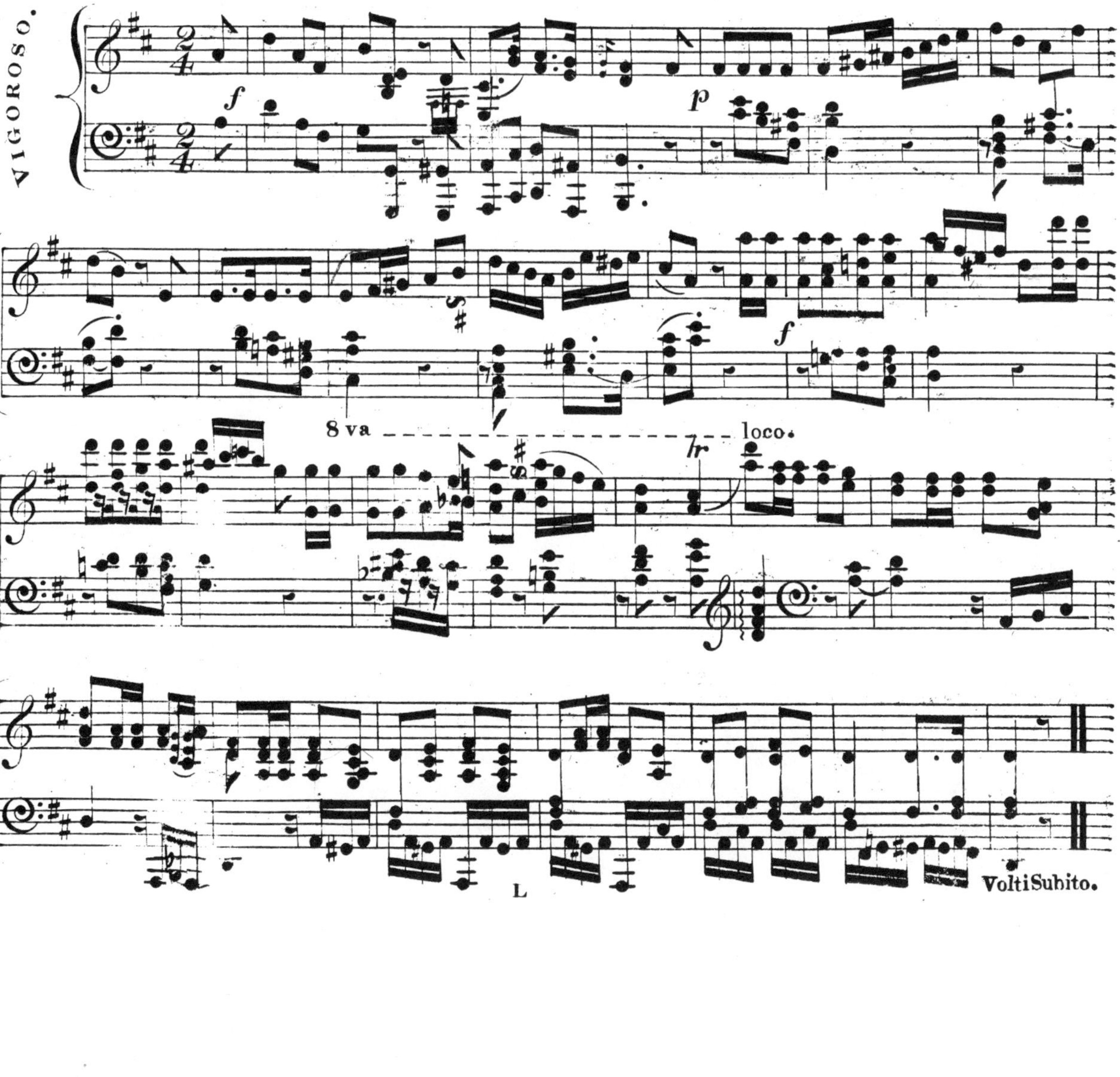
VIGOROSO.
f
p
f
8va
loco.
tr
Volti Subito.

All hail! to Ken=tucky and long may she be,
tr
A re=fuge for want and th'a=bode of the free,
What tongue can ex=press all her beauties sub=lime, Or tell in the
world of so matchless a clime.
con forza:

What tongue can express all her
beauties sub = lime, Or tell in the world of so matchless a clime.
With her forests so wild = = = and rivers so clear.

And her wide fertile fields that load the rich year,
And the lords of her soil so gen' = rous and brave, That give wel = =
sf
come to strangers, to foe = men a grave.
And the lords of her soil so

gen'= rous and brave That give welcome to stran=gers to foe = men a grave.
con Licenza.
p
And then her fair daughters un=ri =vall'd that shine O'er scenes so ely=sian in beau = ty di=

= vine.
And bright glowing youths all their beauties to feel, In
Peace made of love but in War all of steel. And bright glowing youths all their beauties to
feel, In Peace made of love but in War all of steel.
f

p
CODA.
Then where is the
un poco piu Adagio piu tosto ad lib;
land on this earth that the Sun Can with beam so im=

passion'd or bright shine = = up = on.

ad lib: a Tempo. *f*

FINIS.

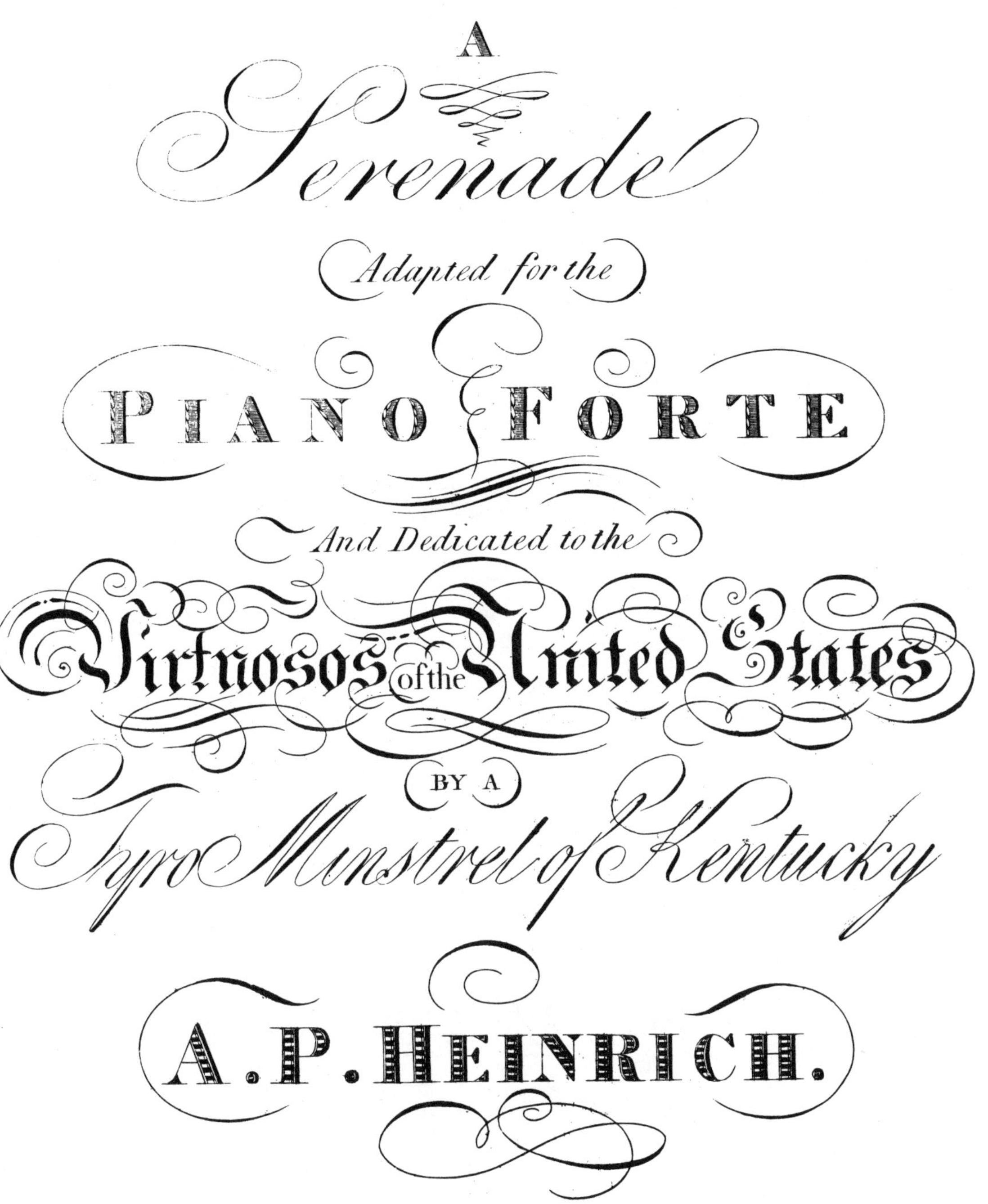
A

Serenade

Adapted for the

PIANO FORTE

And Dedicated to the

Virtuosos of the United States

BY A

Tyro Minstrel of Kentucky

A. P. HEINRICH.

Pr. 75.

PHILADELPHIA, PUBLISHED BY BACON & HART, AND BY
THE AUTHOR, KENTUCKY.

SERENATA.

Vi sa=lu=to con Diffi=den=za ma con A=mo= = re.
ALLA MARCIA
ALLEGRAMENTE.
mf
dol.
8va
loco.
scivolando con un deto.
8va
loco.
8va
sf

8va
un poco ad libitum.
sf
sf
sf
sf

ALLA TRIO.
Scherzando.
8va
loco
espress:

p
f
p
ff
8va
loco
CODA.
risoluto.
grazioso.

molto espress:
1st
2d
ff
poco Adagio ma con molto Espress: e Dolc:
tr
veloce e forte
Tornando la Destra si alza a piacere per andar a Letto.
Bona Notte Buo = = nissima Not = = = te

1

SONATA

A. P. HEINRICH.

Pr: 1,25.

PHILADELPHIA, PUBLISHED BY BACON & HART, AND BY
THE AUTHOR, KENTUCKY.

A SONATA FOR THE PIANO FORTE.

Especially dedicated to the VIRTUOSOS of the United States; not as a NON PLUS ULTRA or NOLI ME TANGERE but as a "firstling" in its kind from the BACK-WOODS and as a small Morning's Entertainment or "BUONA MATTINA" in addition to the SERENADE or "BUONA NOTTE", already presented to them by their most humble ——

A. P. HEINRICH, of Kentucky.

un poco ritart:

Accet = ta = te gli Os=sequi d'un povero Figlio d'Or = = = =

ALLA MANIERA GUISTA.

=feo esi = lia = to nelle Selve ed Antri os=

a tempo. ad lib. a tempo. espres:

=cu = ri e sola = mente inspi = ra = to dagli Concen = = ti

dolce. con Licenza.

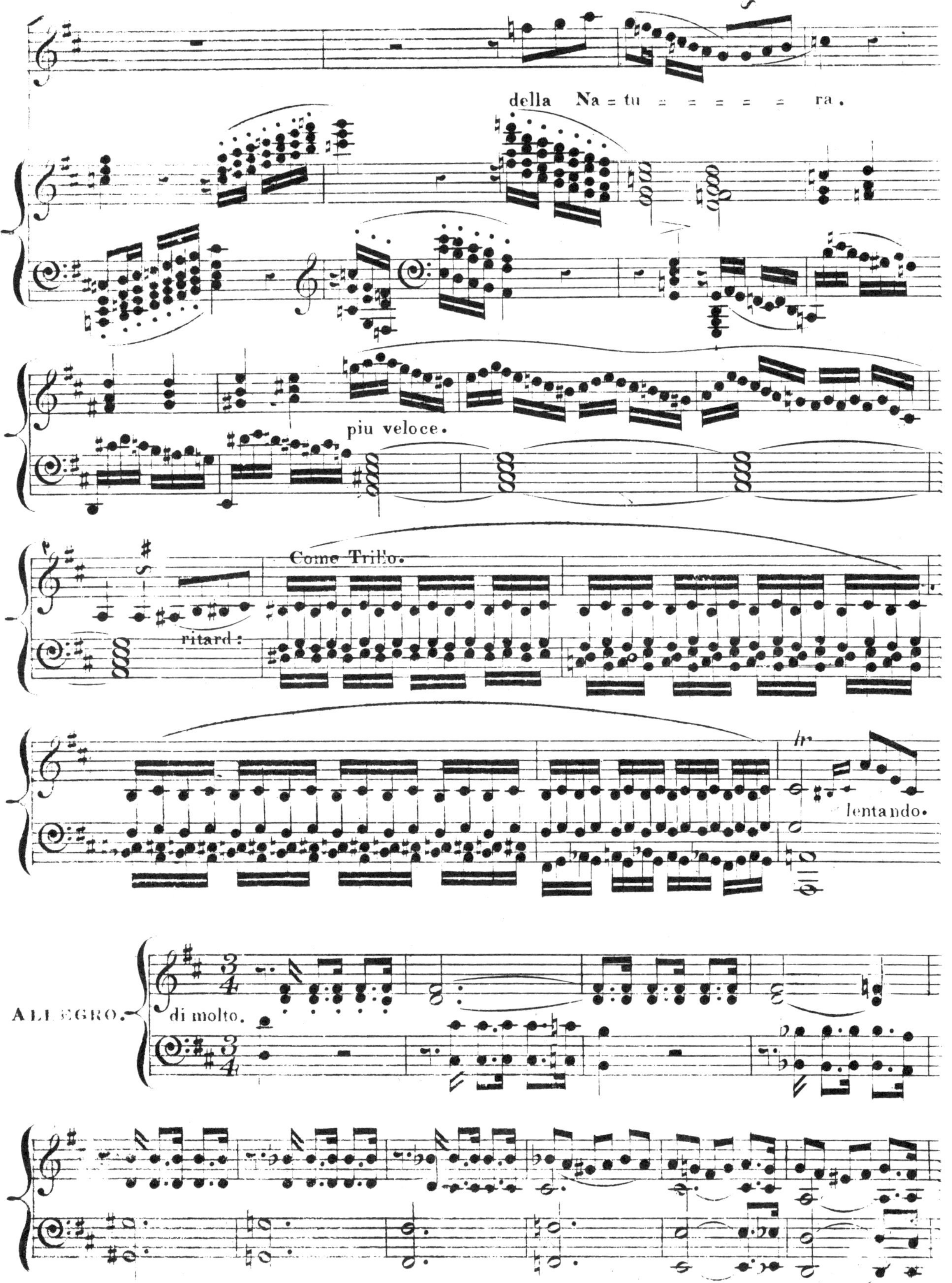
della Na = tu = = = = = ra.
piu veloce.
Come Trillo.
ritard:
lentando.
ALLEGRO.
di molto.

tr
espress:
grazioso.
espress:
rf

espress: e dol:
ff

mf
grazioso:
f
cres:

77140

dol.
cres:
tr
crest
1st
2d
3
Tocca subito l'Andante

ANDANTE
PIU TOSTO
ADAGIO.
p
cres:
espress:
dol:
espress:
p
espres:
dol.
cres:
p
pp
cres:
calando.
p
espress:
con grazia:

un poco ad libitum.
Finale alla Polacca.
Grazioso.
8va.
loco:
dol:
espress:

tr
dol:
mf
con grazia:
espress:
3
3
3
3
f
loco:
8va

ff
piu dol:
8 va.
loco:
ff
dol:
8 va.
loco

CODA.
rf
rf
rit.
a tempo.
f
ritart:
Ca = ri A = mi = ci = vi a = u = gu = ro sempre fe = li = cissi = mi gior = ni, Addi = o !

A BOTTLE SONG,

The Verses by

The Music for the

Piano Forte & Voices,

BY

A. P. HEINRICH,

And Inscribed as a Coup d'Essai to

 Pr. 75.

PHILADELPHIA, PUBLISHED BY BACON & HART AND BY

THE AUTHOR KENTUCKY.

J

SIX BUMPERS — SEMPRE CRESCENDO.
ANACREONTIC.
Nº 1.
rallentº
Il canto solo —
Ecco il Piano Forte.
No Churchman am I for to rail and to write, No
Statesman nor Sol = dier to plot or to fight, No sly man of
busi = ness con = tri = ving a snare, For a big bel = ly'd bot = tle's the
whole of my care.

J

Volti

Nº 2.
The Peer I don't en = vy I give him his bow I scorn not the
MINORE.
Peasant tho' ev = er so low
But a club of good fel = lows like those that are
here And a bottle like this are my glo = ry and care
Nº 3.
Here passes the Squire on his
MAGGIORE.
broth = er his horse There Cent = um per cent = um the

sf
Cit with his purse, But see you the Crown how it waves in the
air, There a big belly'd bottle still ea = ses my care.
Nº 4.
The wife of my bosom a = las! she did
MINORE.
die, For sweet con = so = la = tion to church I did fly, I found that old
Solo = mon proved it fair, That a big bel = ly'd bottle's a cure for all

care.
Nº 5.
I once was persuaded a ven = ture to
MAGGIORE:
make, A let = ter in = = form'd me that all was to
wreck, But the pursy old Landlord just waddled up stairs, With a
glo = = ri = ous bottle that en = ded my cares.

Nº 6.
Life's cares they are comforts a max=im laid down By the
MINORE.
Bard what d'ye call him that wore the black gown And faith! I a=gree with the old
prig to a hair, For a big bel=ly'd bot=tle's a heaven of care.
8va
Bene Placito.

AN OVERFLOWING BUMPER, ADDED, TO THE MEMORY OF THE MASONIC VIRTUOSO ROBERT BURNS.

Square Have a big bel = ly'd bot = tle when har = ass'd with care.
Square Have a big bel = ly'd bot=tle when har = ass'd with care.
Square Have a big bel = ly'd bot=tle when har = ass'd with care.
8 va
loco.
legato:
8 va
loco.
8 va:
CODA TOPS
IN TURVA O
AD LIBITUM

POSTSCRIPT — OR A HEALTH TO AMATEURS

VALSO CANTANTE.

MAGGIORE.
IL CANTO MINORE
SINFONIA MAGGIORE.
ff
Il Walz da Capo, ma senza
l'Introduzione, dopo l'ultimo Verso
si conclude a piacere.

The Young Columbian Midshipman,

A Waltz Song

Written by

H. C. LEWIS,

Composed by

A. P. Heinrich.

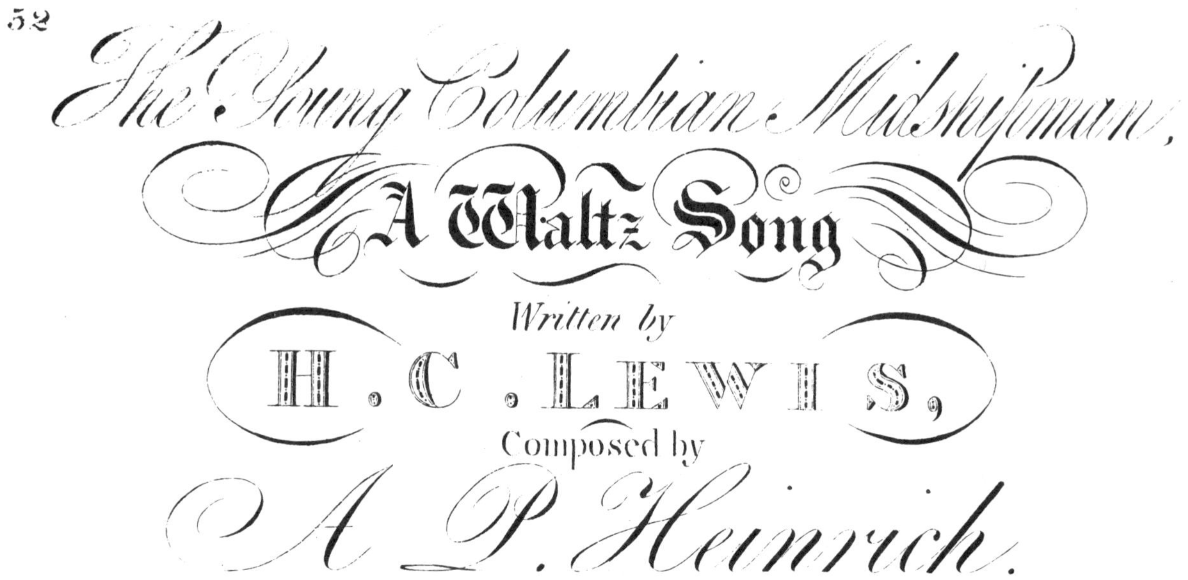

Pr: 25.

Philadelphia Published by BACON & HART and by the AUTHOR Kentucky.

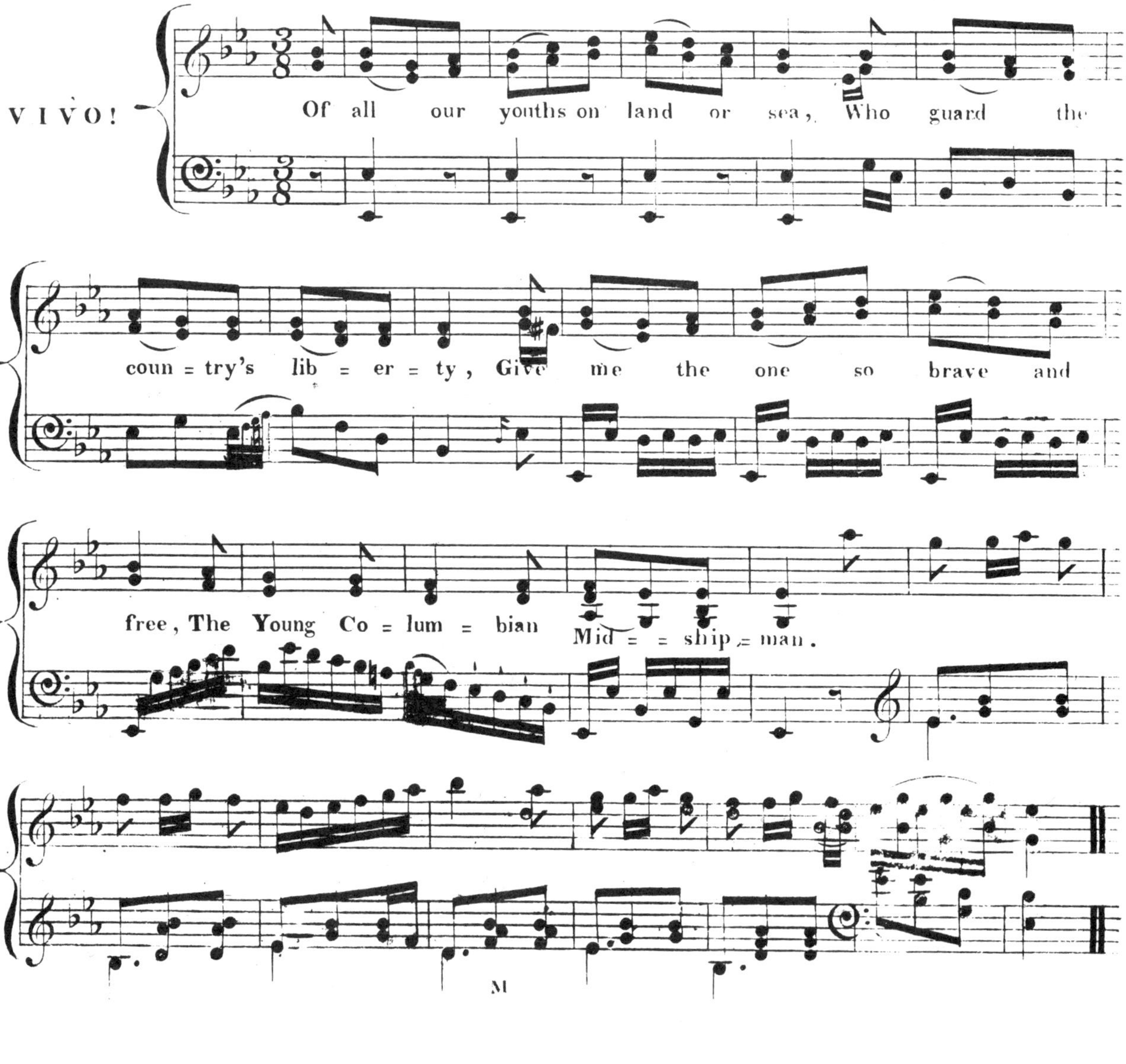
VIVO!
Of all our youths on land or sea, Who guard the
coun = try's lib = er = ty, Give me the one so brave and
free, The Young Co = lum = bian Mid = = ship = man.

He's first in war the foe to dare, He's first in love to
con espressione.
win the fair, With him no one can I com = pare, The
Young Co = lum = bian Mid = = ship = man.
ff
Canto D.C.

When call'd to duty on the main,
He scorns delay,(our tears are vain,)
But swears soon to return again,
The Young Columbian Midshipman!

When ev'ry cannon's echoing roar,
Gives glory to his native shore,
And honest laurels deck him o'er,
The Young &c.

His country serv'd, then friend or fair,
Engages all his gallant care,
And conquers both in peace or war,
The Young &c.

Let smiles increase his patriot flame,
All hands entwine his wreath of fame,
And oft be sung his deathless fame,
The Young &c.

EPITOME.

CANTO.

8va.

8va.

LORD BYRON'S COTILLION.*

FOR THE PIANO FORTE — AN EXTRACT FROM "THE FAIR HAYDÉE"

A SONG WRITTEN BY THAT EMINENT ENGLISH BARD,

AND COMPOSED BY A. P. HEINRICH.

 Pr. 12.

Philadelphia Published by BACON & HART, and by the AUTHOR, Kentucky.

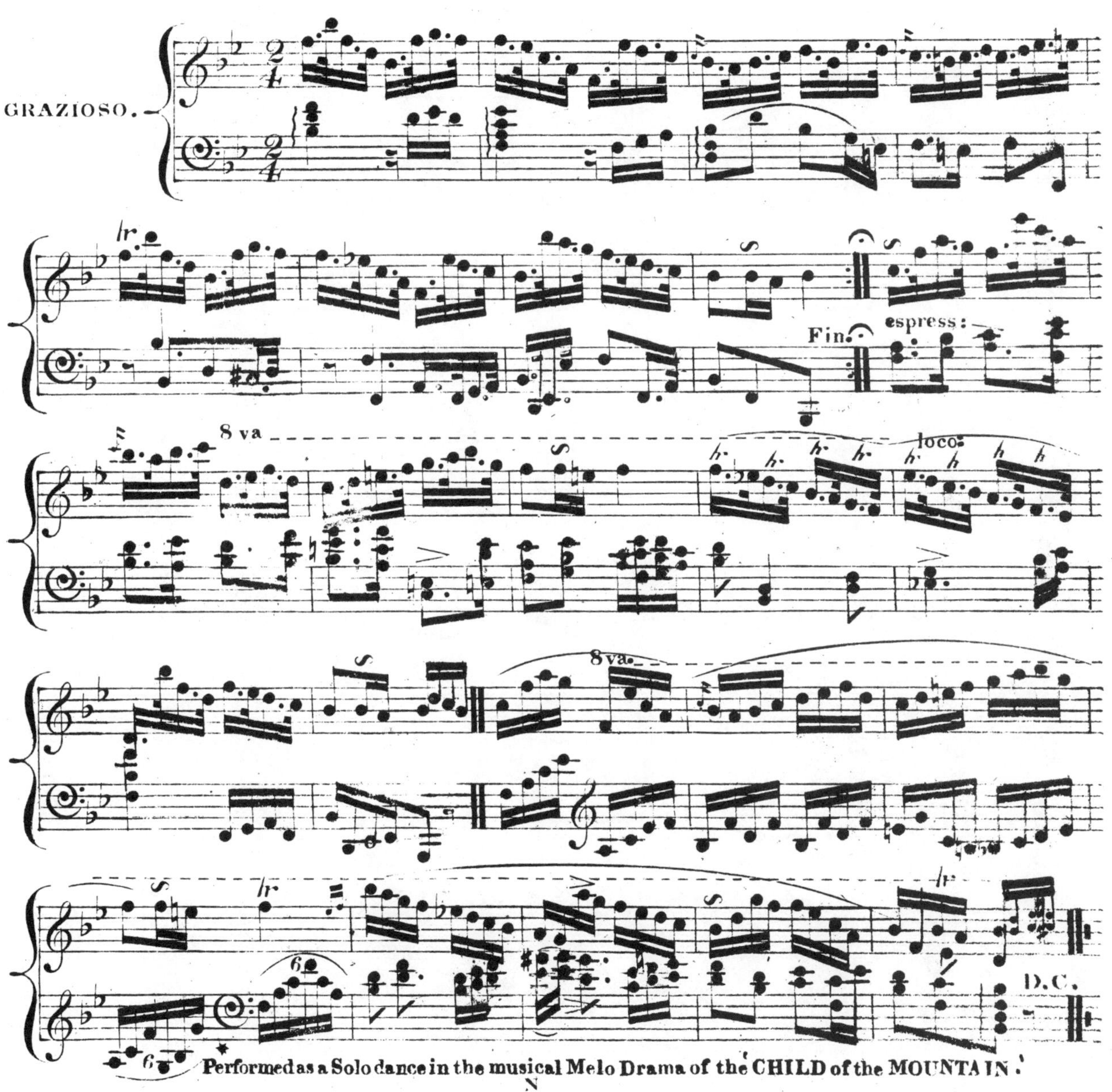

* Performed as a Solo dance in the musical Melo Drama of the CHILD of the MOUNTAIN.

Fair Haïdée's Waltz

COMPOSED BY A. P. HEINRICH.

 Pr: 12

RONDO WALTZ, for the Piano Forte,

Composed by

A. P. HEINRICH.

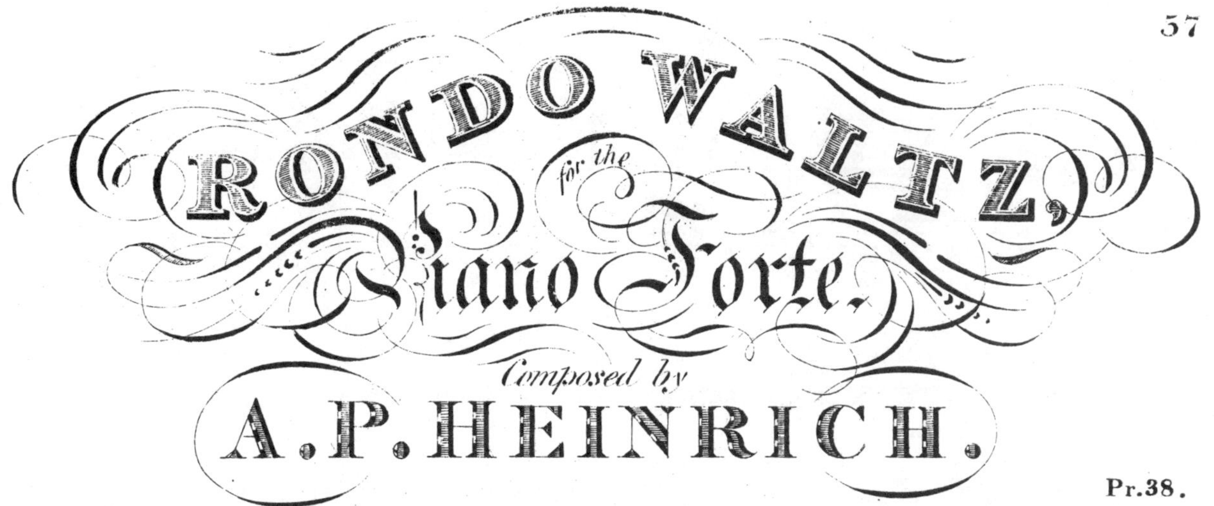

Pr. 38.

PHILADELPHIA, Published by BACON & HART, and by the AUTHOR, Kentucky.

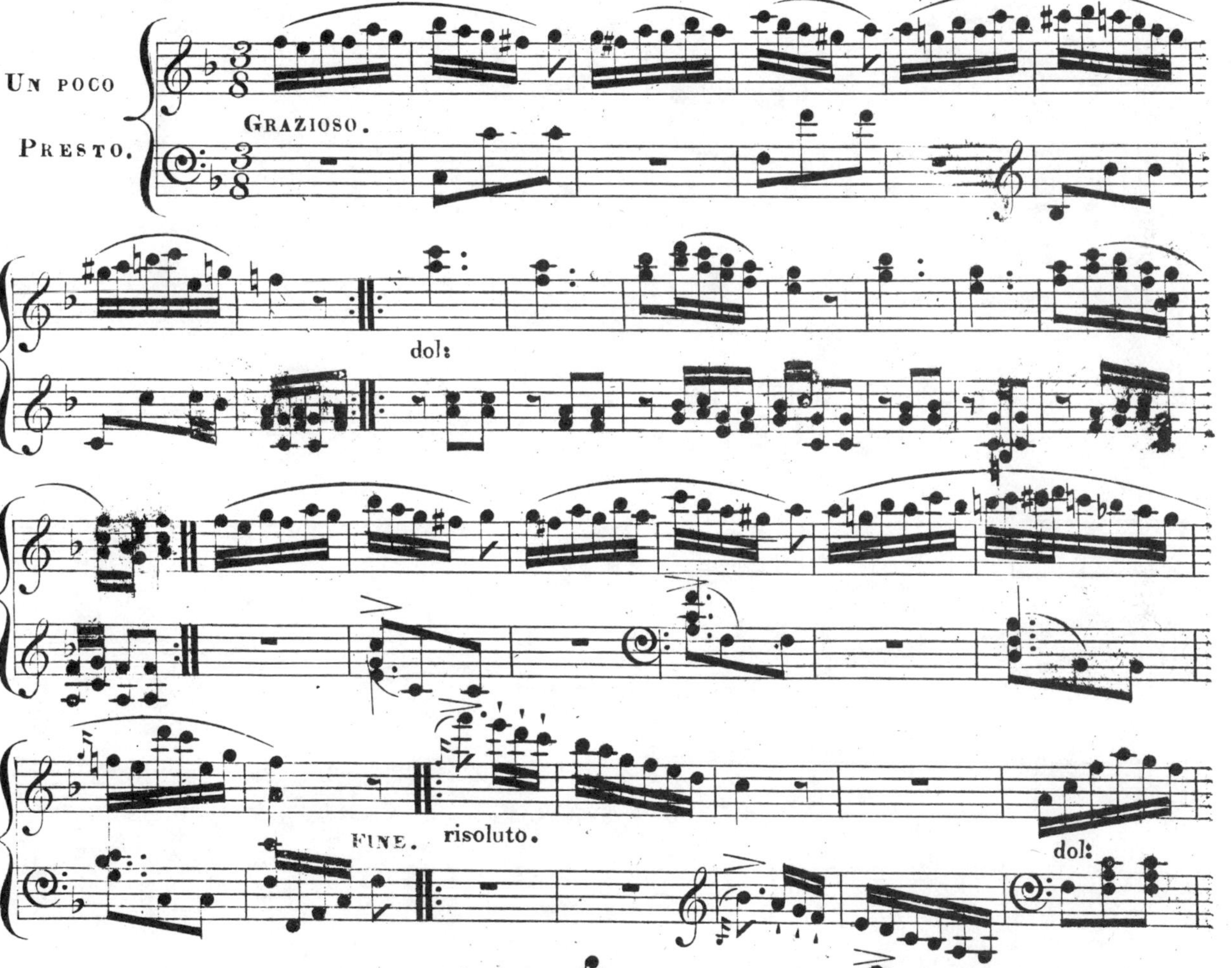
Un poco Presto.
Grazioso.
dol:
Fine.
risoluto.
dol:
cres:
espress:

mf
dol:
rf.
mf
dol:
espress:
dol:
tr

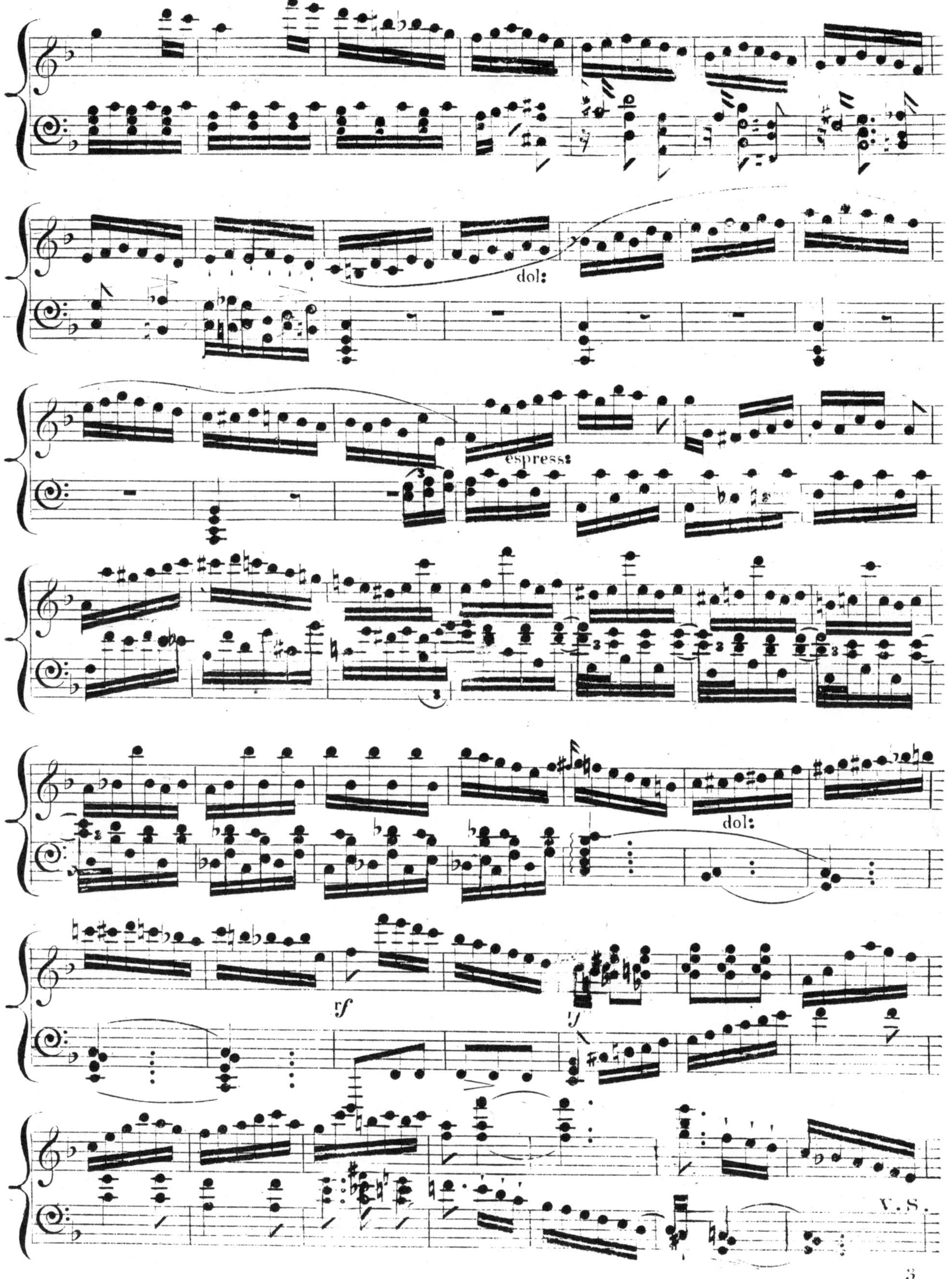
dol:
espress:
dol:
rf
V. S.

espress:
dol:
dol:
crescendo.
D.C.

 Pr. 50.

PHILADELPHIA, Published by BACON & HART, and by the AUTHOR, Kentucky.

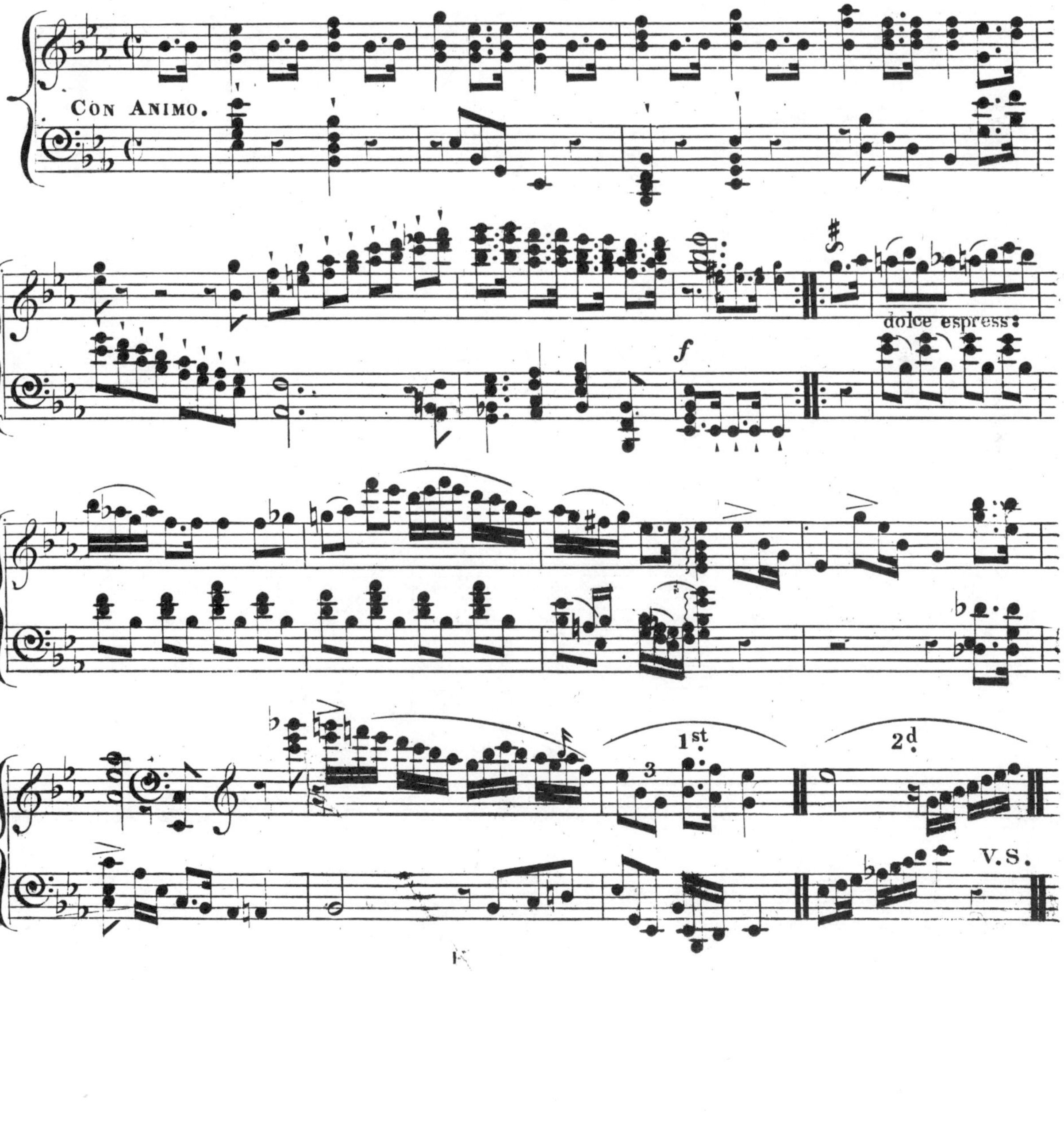

Con Animo.

f

dolce espress:

1st

2d

3

V.S.

espress.

espress.

calando:

f

6

6

6

dol e espress:

cres.

8 va.

F

sf

TRIO.
S.
GRAZIOSO.
S.
espress:
espress:
c.L.
S.
S.
p
espress:
legato.
rit.

UN POCO
PRESTO.
GRAZIOSO.
cres:

dol:

FINIS.

WITH AN ACCOMPANIMENT FOR THE FLUTE OR VIOLIN,

AND DEDICATED TO HIS FRIEND

 Pr. 38

PHILADELPHIA, Published by BACON & HART, and by the AUTHOR, Kentucky.

THE MUSICAL BACHELOR.

fair = = est lass, That ev = er swayed on beau = = ty's throne; Un=
p
dolce:
espress:
= less her heart like mir = ror'd glass, My ev' = ry feel = ing, pas = sion,
dolce.
espress:
espress:
shone.
espress:

2
I would not wed the wittiest maid,
That ever touch'd a mortals heart;
Unless her darts were merely played,
In simple innocency's part.

3
I would not wed the purest soul,
That ever feeling govern'd most;
Unless her heart would bear control,
And of its goodness never boast.

4
I would not wed, else perfect being,
If she but wanted music's taste;
To it I should fore'er be fleeing,
And find at home a dreary waste.

HAIL COLUMBIA!

Minuet

Composed by

A. P. HEINRICH.

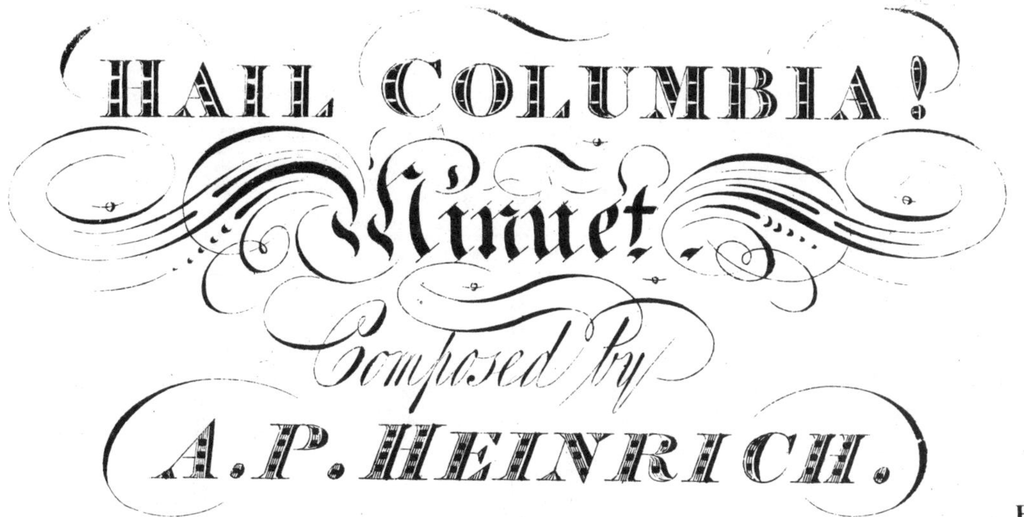

Pr. 25.

PHILADELPHIA, Published by BACON & HART, and by the AUTHOR, Kentucky.

INTRODUZIONE

ALLA TROMBO.

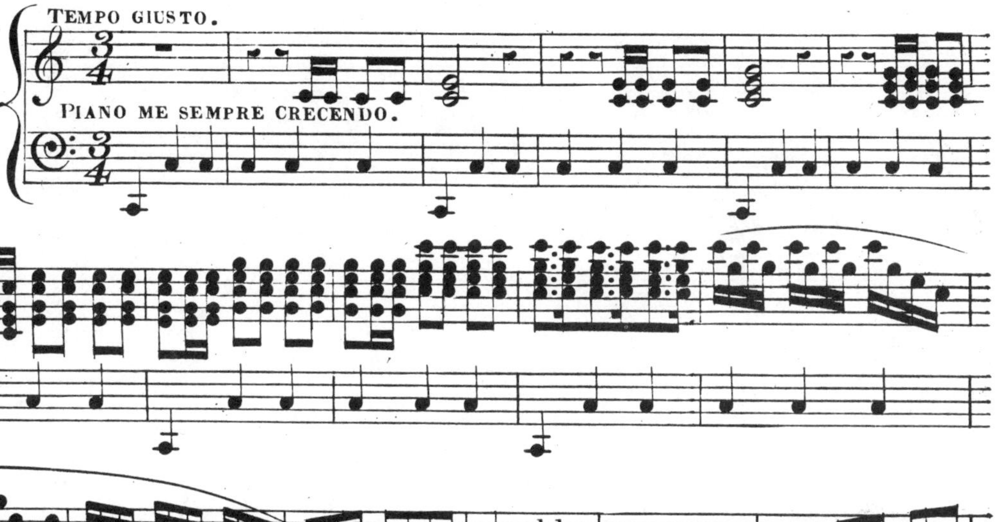
TEMPO GIUSTO.
PIANO ME SEMPRE CRECENDO.
dolce.
MINUETTO.
rf
rf
dols
V.S.

dol:
espress°
alla Trio:
in vece del DA CAPO.
dol:
espress°.
dol:
dol:

The foregoing Menuet & the following Yankee Doodle Waltz have been adapted by the Author as an Overture to a new Farce call'd the Authors Night under the title of the COLUMBIAD. 3

YANKEE DOODLE, Waltz,

COMPOSED BY

A. P. HEINRICH.

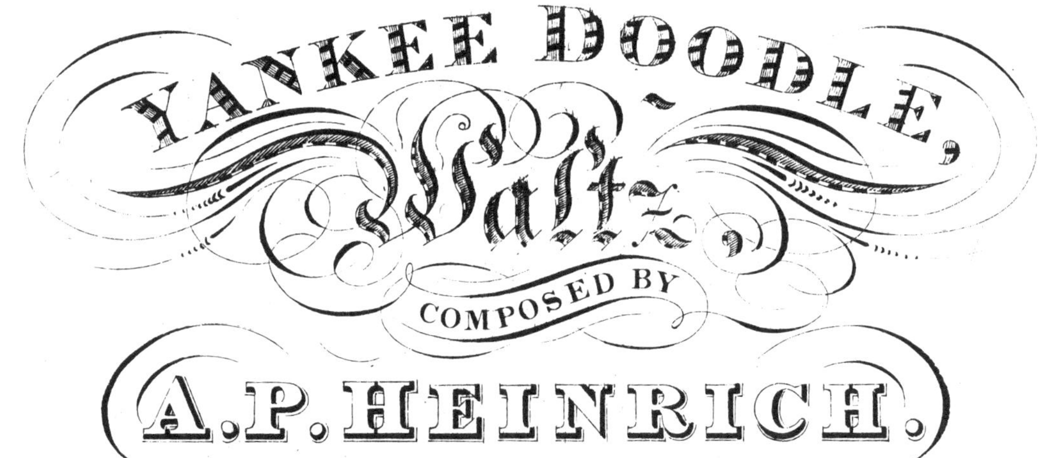

Pr. 25.

PHILADELPHIA, Published by BACON & HART, and by the AUTHOR, Kentucky.

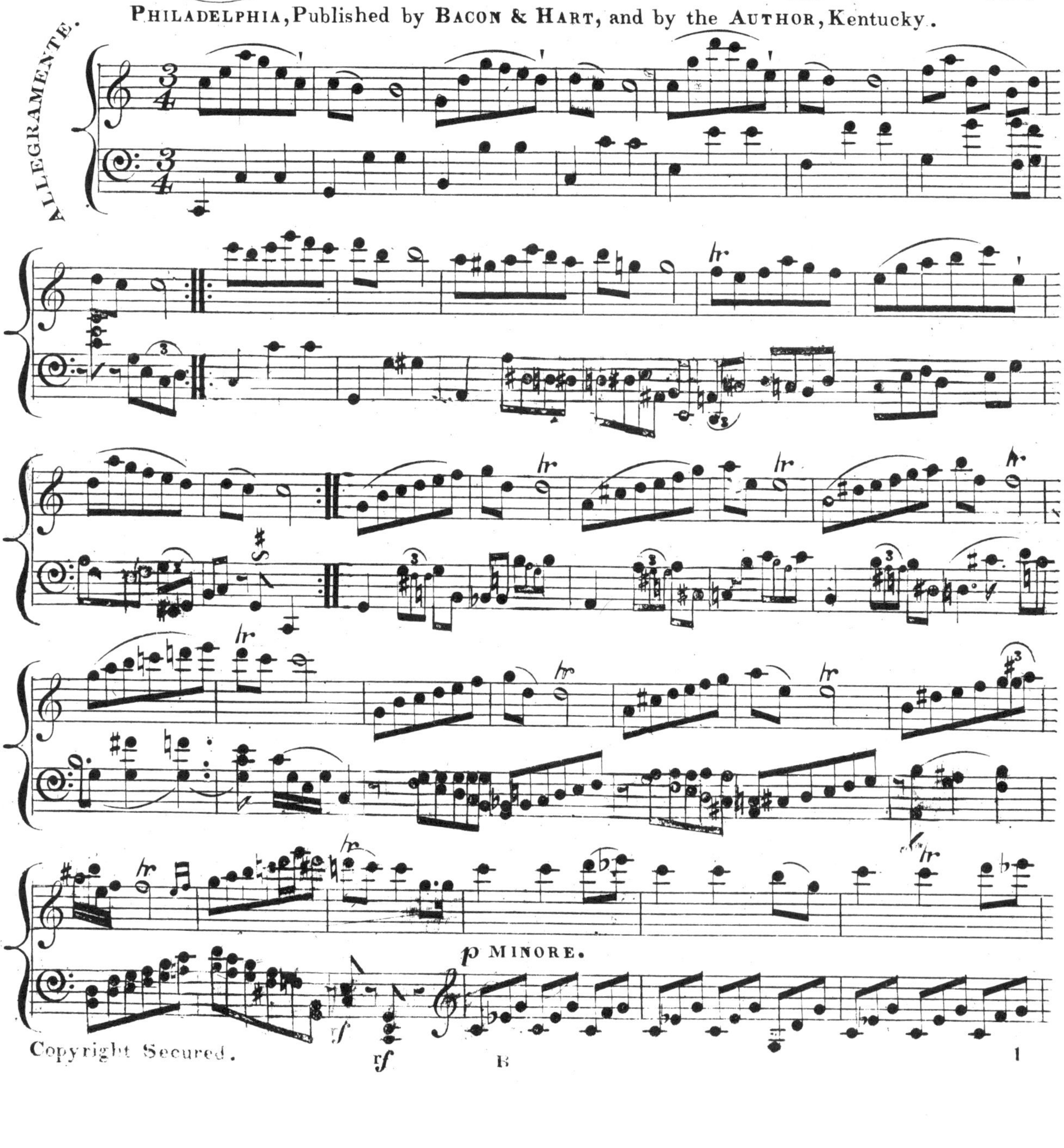
ALLEGRAMENTE.
tr
p MINORE.
rf

MAGGIORE.
f
ff
Grazioso.

CODA.
Piu vivo, quasi Presto.
ff
p
bis
cres.

ODE BY COLLINS.

How sleep the Brave,

The Music

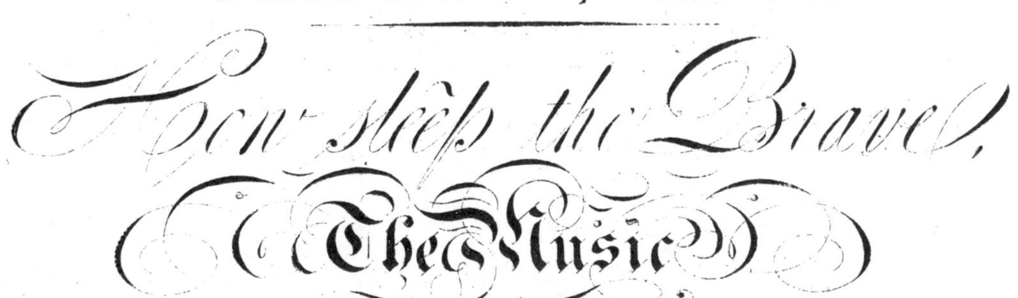

COMPOSED AT THE REQUEST OF SEVERAL LADIES OF BARDSTOWN, KY. IN COMMEMORATION OF THE HEROES WHO FELL AT TIPPECANOE AND THE RIVER RAISIN,

BY

A. P. Heinrich,

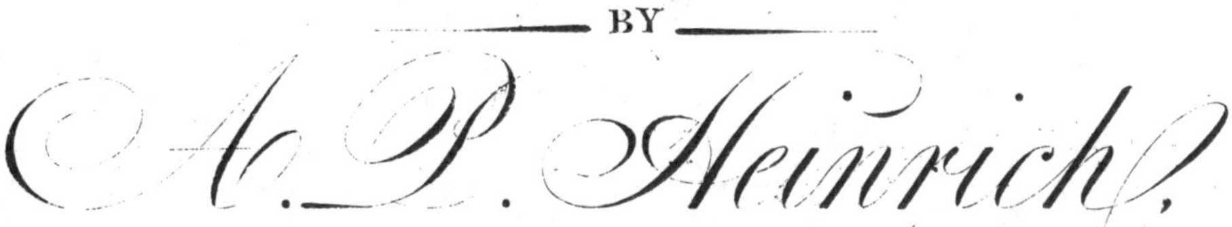

 Pr. 25.

PHILADELPHIA, Published by BACON & HART, and by the AUTHOR, Kentucky.

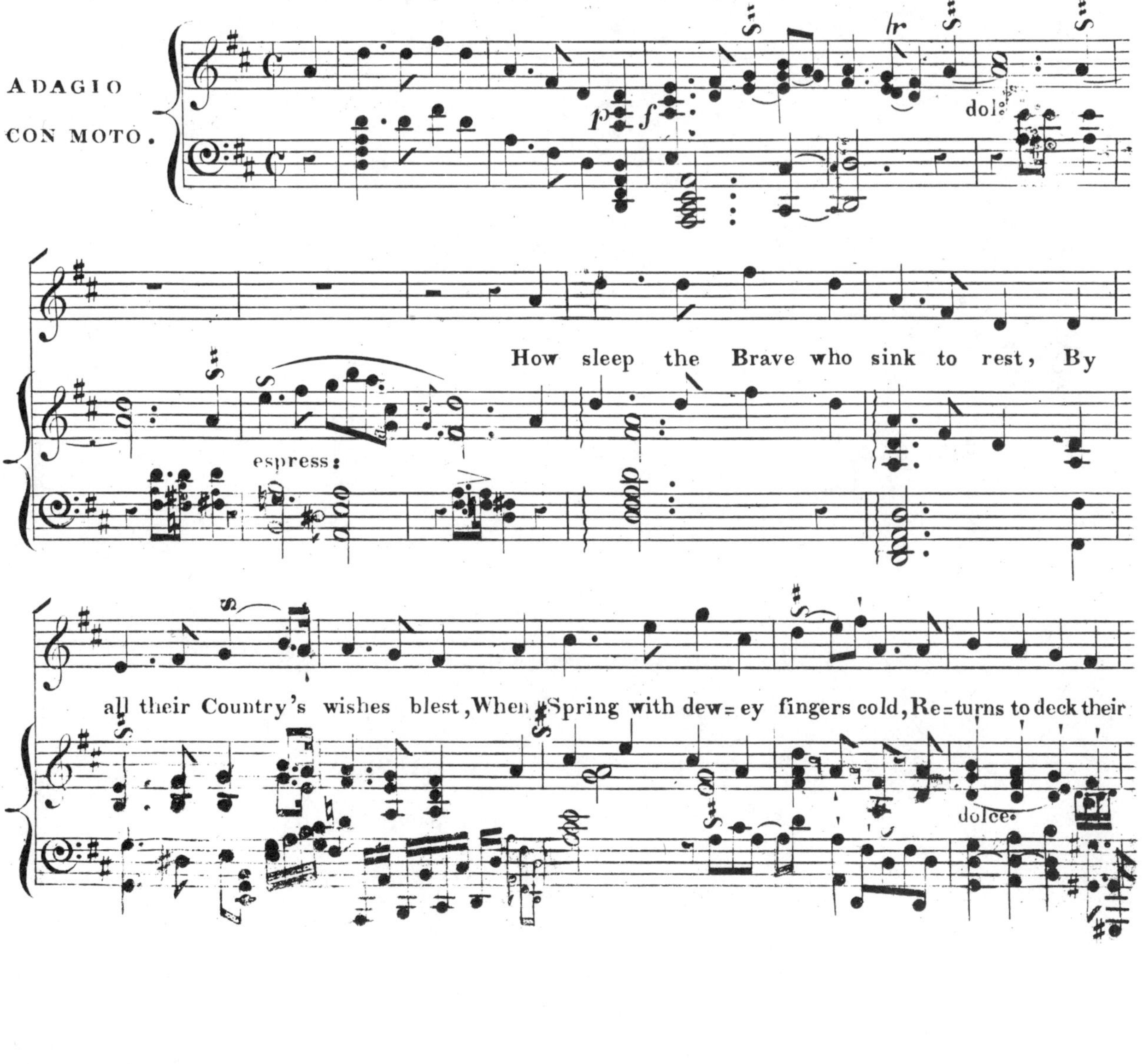

ADAGIO
CON MOTO.
p
f
dol:
espress:
How sleep the Brave who sink to rest, By
all their Country's wishes blest, When Spring with dew= ey fingers cold, Re= turns to deck their
dolce

2

By Fairy hands their knell is rung,
By forms unseen their dirge is sung.
There, Honour comes a Pilgrim grey,
To bless the turf that wraps their clay,
And Freedom shall a while repair,
To dwell a weeping Hermit there.

HARMONIZED FOR THREE VOICES.

* Optional

The Prague Waltz

COMPOSED BY A. P. HEINRICH. Pr 12.

A COTILLION, FOR THE PIANO FORTE, COMPOSED BY A. P. HEINRICH.

Pr:12.

ALLEGRETTO.

grazioso.

8.

FINIS.

mf

MINORE.

legato e espress:

MAGGIORE.

dol:

cres:

dol:

D.C.

S.

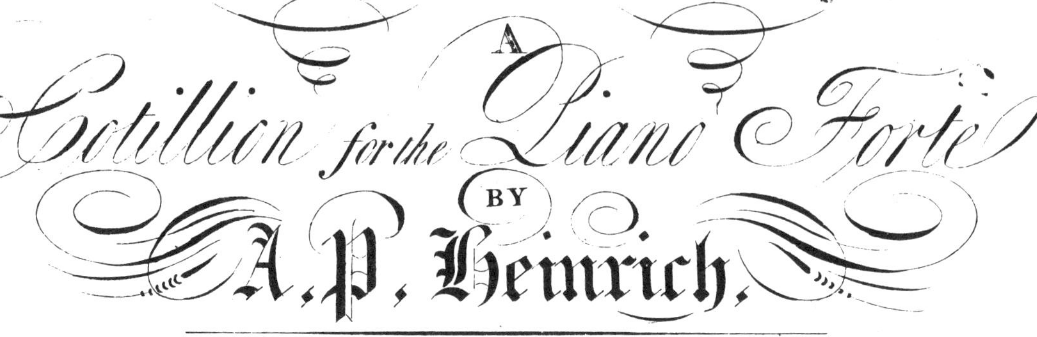

COMPOSED AS A COUNTERPART TO "THE AMIABLE," A FRENCH AIR, WELL KNOWN AND MUCH ADMIRED IN THE BALL-ROOMS OF KENTUCKY.

 Pr: 25.

Philadelphia, Published by BACON & HART, and by the AUTHOR, Kentucky.

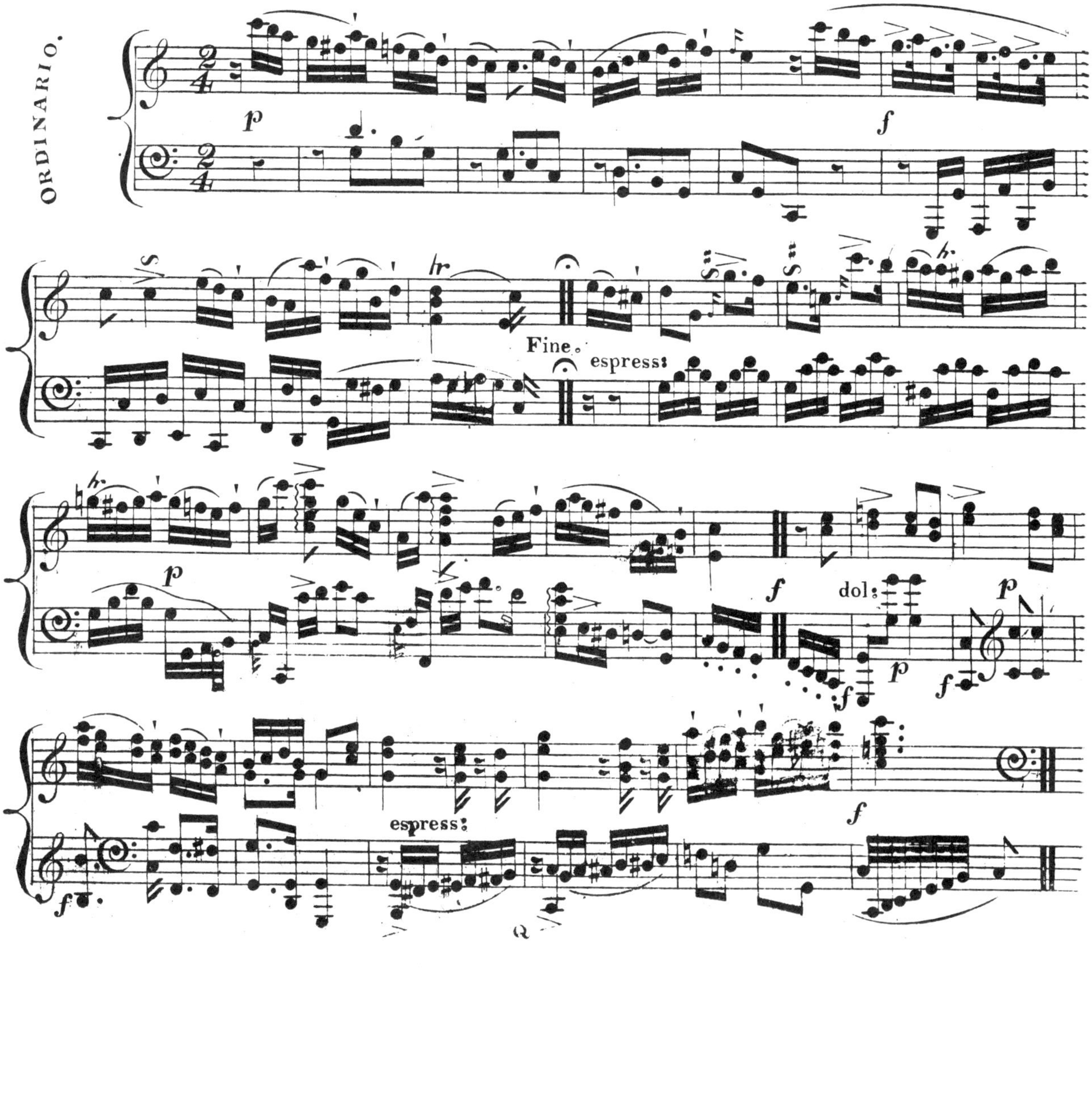

ORDINARIO.

p f Fine. espress: p f dol: p f p f espress: f

A GERMAN HOPSASSA DANCE — BY A. P. HEINRICH.

ALLEGRETTO.

p

f

AN ALLEMANDE. BY A. P. HEINRICH.

A PATRIOTIC ODE.

THE POETRY FROM THE NATIONAL INTELLIGENCER.* THE MUSIC, COMPOSED, WITH AN ACCOMPANIMENT FOR THE PIANO FORTE, AT THE REQUEST OF THE HON. JUDGE SPEED, OF FARMINGTON, (LOUISVILLE, KY.) TO WHOM, AND TO AN INDULGENT PUBLIC, IT IS MOST RESPECTFULLY PRESENTED, BY THEIR DEVOTED FELLOW CITIZEN, A. P. HEINRICH.

* It is with regret, that A. P. Heinrich has to publish the following Music without inserting the Name of the Author of the Poetry.— He can only add, that from repeated inquiries at the Office of the National Intelligencer, he could not gain the desired information.

The Composer trusts, that the Melody throughout, will be found smooth and flowing, and well adapted for the Flute and Violin:— Should the Piano Forte accompaniment, prove difficult, the same is left ad Libitum.

 Pr. 62.

Philadelphia, Published by BACON & HART, and by the AUTHOR, Kentucky.

dol:
Im= mortal Chief ! whose matchless deeds pro claim, The hero's glory & the statesman's fame, Whose
worth at=tested by thy country's voice, Ob=tain'd her suffrage and confirm'd her choice, In
war her leader and in peace her guide, And first in both her bulwark and her pride, To

thy great name, on this auspicious day, A grateful people heartfelt homage pay. They
bless that name, to truth and freedom dear, And give to WASHINGTON the patriot tear; To
him, whose sword a-chiev'd his country's cause, whose rule maintain'd her liberty and laws,
sf
s

Whose noble mind no venom'd slander knew, Whose
warrior arm no poison'd weapon drew, Whose onward path to glory's summit led, While ev'ry
vir = tue beam'd around his head, Whose pi = ous step approach'd religion's fane — No
vile polytheist, no sceptic vain, Whose glorious life the bright ex=ample gave, The proud to

humble and the vanquish'd save, Whose death serene a better world confess'd, When
passing tranquil, to e = ternal rest; To him Co=lumbia's grat = itude be given, Her guardian
here, her advocate in heaven. To him Columbia's gratitude, Co=lumbia's gratitude be
given, Her guardian here her ad = vo = cate in heav = = = = en.
dol:

S

un poco piu svegliato.
p

TO THE MEMORY OF

COMMODORE O.H. PERRY,

 Pr.: 38.

Philadelphia, Published by BACON & HART, and by the AUTHOR, Kentucky.

The above Music is an extract from "The funeral strains" of the Author, A.P. Heinrich — As they have been indulgently recieved in private circles, he would venture to give this Requiem to the Public, as a token of respect for the memory of the departed Hero. —

T

PER = RY! now no more! Let tears be = dew his sacred grave, While
doloroso.
fame at = tends the good and brave! — Im = mor = tal as the skies. The
Flauto
Legato.
fav = 'rite he = ro dies, And Freedom mourns her dearest son, her dearest son, While
Flauto.
Vict'ry points to all he won! — Tho' nought avails a na = tion's woe, (It

ne'er re = calls the he = ro gone,) Yet tears from ev = 'ry
free = man flow, And "Beauty weeps herself to stone!" Oh! PER = RY! hallow'd
Corni
name! E = ter = nal is thy fame! And blest thy
ff
p
Flauto.
death! for now thou'rt gone To dwell in heav'n with WASHING = TON.
legato.

E P I, T O M E.

FOR THE PIANO FORTE AND ALSO FOR THE VIOLIN OR FLUTE.

Fine.

Da Capo.

Da Capo.

Columbia's Plaint.

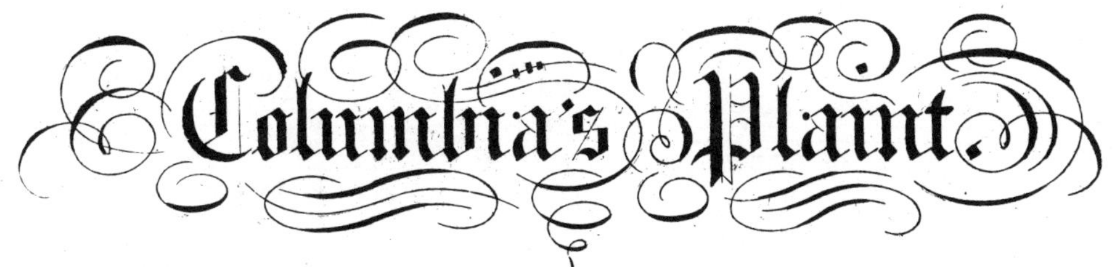

WRITTEN BY H. C. LEWIS, AND RESPECTFULLY DEDICATED TO HIS

MASONIC BRETHREN,*

THE MUSIC COMPOSED, BY A. P. HEINRICH, AND CALCULATED TO BE EASILY HARMONIZED FOR TWO, OR THREE VOICES, OR SIMPLIFIED "A GUSTO."

---

*It is a fact, that Washington, Hamilton, Lawrence, Perry, Burrows, Bush, and indeed a large majority of the departed Officers of the Army and Navy, and of the signers of the Declaration of the American Independence, were members of the Ancient Order.

 Pr: 25

Philadelphia, Published by BACON & HART, and by the Author, Kentucky.

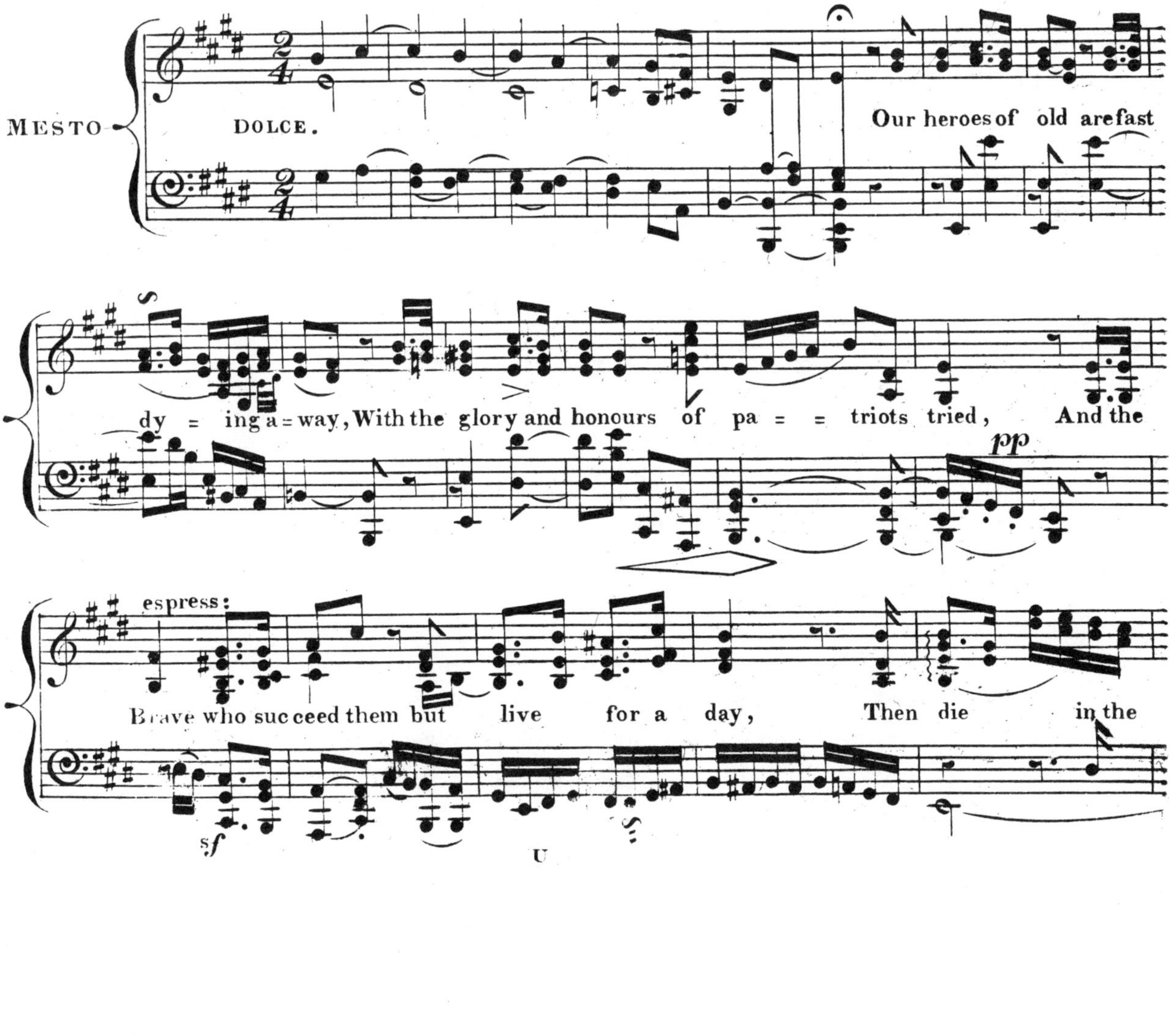
MESTO
DOLCE.
Our heroes of old are fast
dy = ing a = way, With the glory and honours of pa = = triots tried, And the
pp
espress:
Brave who succeed them but live for a day, Then die in the
sf

2

The few of the worthies, of Washington's days,
Who remain in the land which their bravery blest,
Are indeed but a few! — and each morrow conveys
A statesman or warrior to glory and rest!

3

Our tears are scarce dry for the warrior slain,
Or the statesman consigned to his halcyon grave,
Ere they flow for some favourite Son of the Main,
A <u>Bush</u>, or a <u>Burrows</u>, a <u>Lawrence</u>, so brave!

SENSIBILITY, AND Sensibility's Child,

TWO ORIGINAL SONGS,

Written by H. C. Lewis, of Phila.[a]

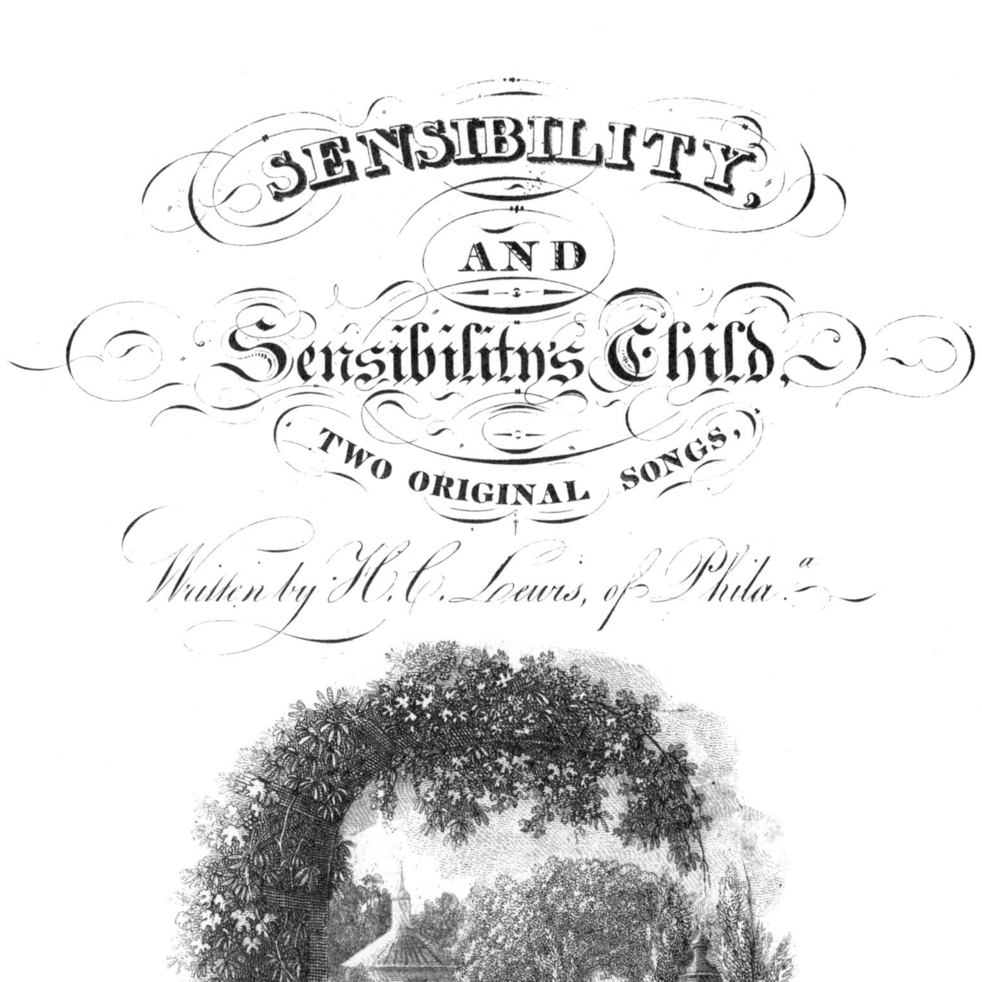

THE MUSIC COMPOSED & DEDICATED TO

Miss Mary Speed, of Farmington, Kentucky, by

A. P. Heinrich.

Pub.[d] By Bacon & Hart Phila.[a] & By the Author K.[y]

Price (Copy Right Secured.) 50 Cts

SENSIBILITY,

HARMONIZED FOR TWO VOICES, THE PIANO FORTE, AND FLUTE;

(THE SECOND VOICE AND FLUTE AD LIBITUM.)

p
O! live in the heart that has bled at your
loco
dolcemente.
dol:
shrine And ever ex = ults with each sensi = tive soul —
espress:
dol:

O! let not your absence once darken my mind,
For a moment with deadliest heart chilling gloom,
But illumine me ever with feelings refin'd,
'Till my life-pulse is o'er and I sink to the tomb.

SENSIBILITY'S CHILD.

2

O! why does he ask when the smile of your eye
Has reveal'd so expressively tender and true,
The sincerest regard for the birth of a sigh,
Which the finest of sensitive hearts ever knew.

3

While bright like the modest, the sun illum'd rose,
Whose fragrance and bloom are so truly refin'd,
The blush of your cheek has ne'er fail'd to disclose
The heart cheering sweet, a fond, diffident mind.

4

And your roseate lips breathing perfumes around,
Which give birth to the words of esteem and regard,
Have prov'd in the mildest, melodious sound,
That you dearly can love the soft Song of the bard.

5

Yes, Mary! each beauty discloses so true,
Your affection, for all that is tender and mild,
That the Bard must indulge in this tribute to you,
And exult, that he's found, Sensibility's Child.

Visit to Farmington.

A COTILLION FOR THE PIANO FORTE AS PERFORMED IN THE BALL ROOMS OF KENTUCKY COMPOSED BY A. P. HEINRICH.

Pr: 12.

The Bride's Farewell

WRITTEN BY HENRY C. LEWIS — COMPOSED BY A. P. HEINRICH.

2

Dear parents, when I'm far from you,
In many a pleasing airy dream,
You and my joys again I'll view,
And absence be my constant theme.
Companions of my youthful years,
Ye girls with whom in mirth I've toy'd,
Of you I'll often think, while tears
Shall bring to mind sports once enjoy'd.

3

Towards a foreign clime I steer,
And should my stars propitious shine,
Perhaps of my return you'll hear,
And I no more in absence pine.
But from this life should I depart,
Ere I return from whence I'm bound,
Mayhap, for me some tender heart,
Will gently heave a sigh profound.

VISIT TO PHILADELPHIA,

THE VERSES BY

H. C. LEWIS,

THE MUSIC COMPOSED FOR THE PIANO FORTE AND VOICE, BY

A. P. Heinrich.

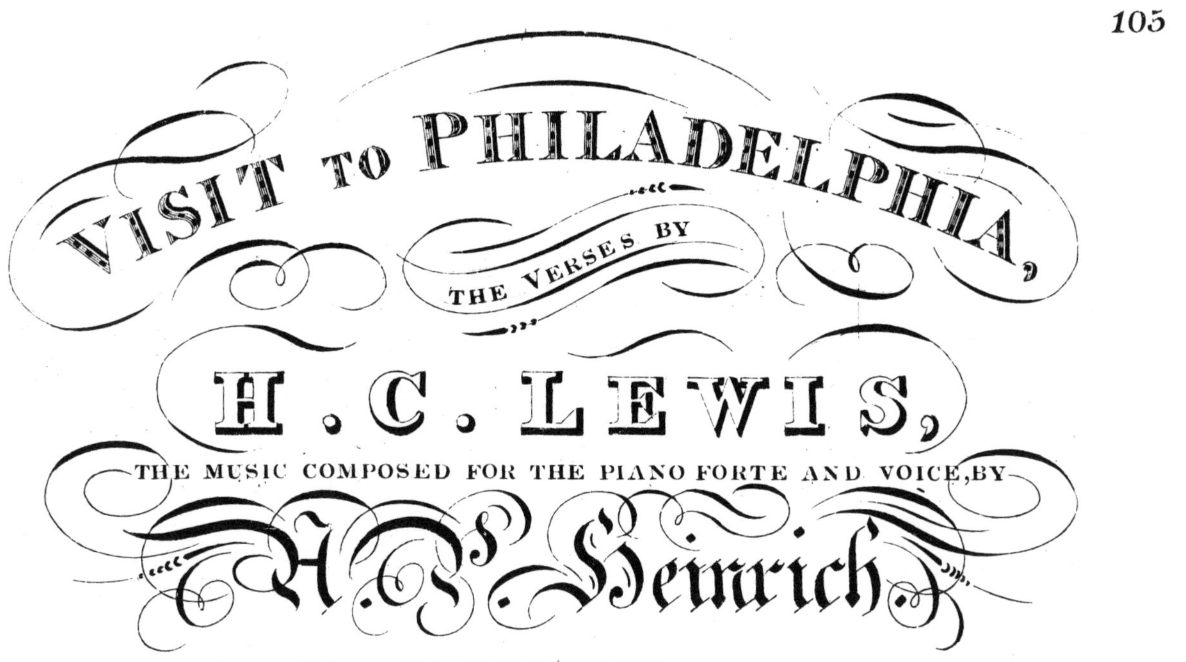

Pr: 100

Philadelphia, Published by BACON & HART, and by the Author, Kentucky.

GUISTO E CON AMORE.

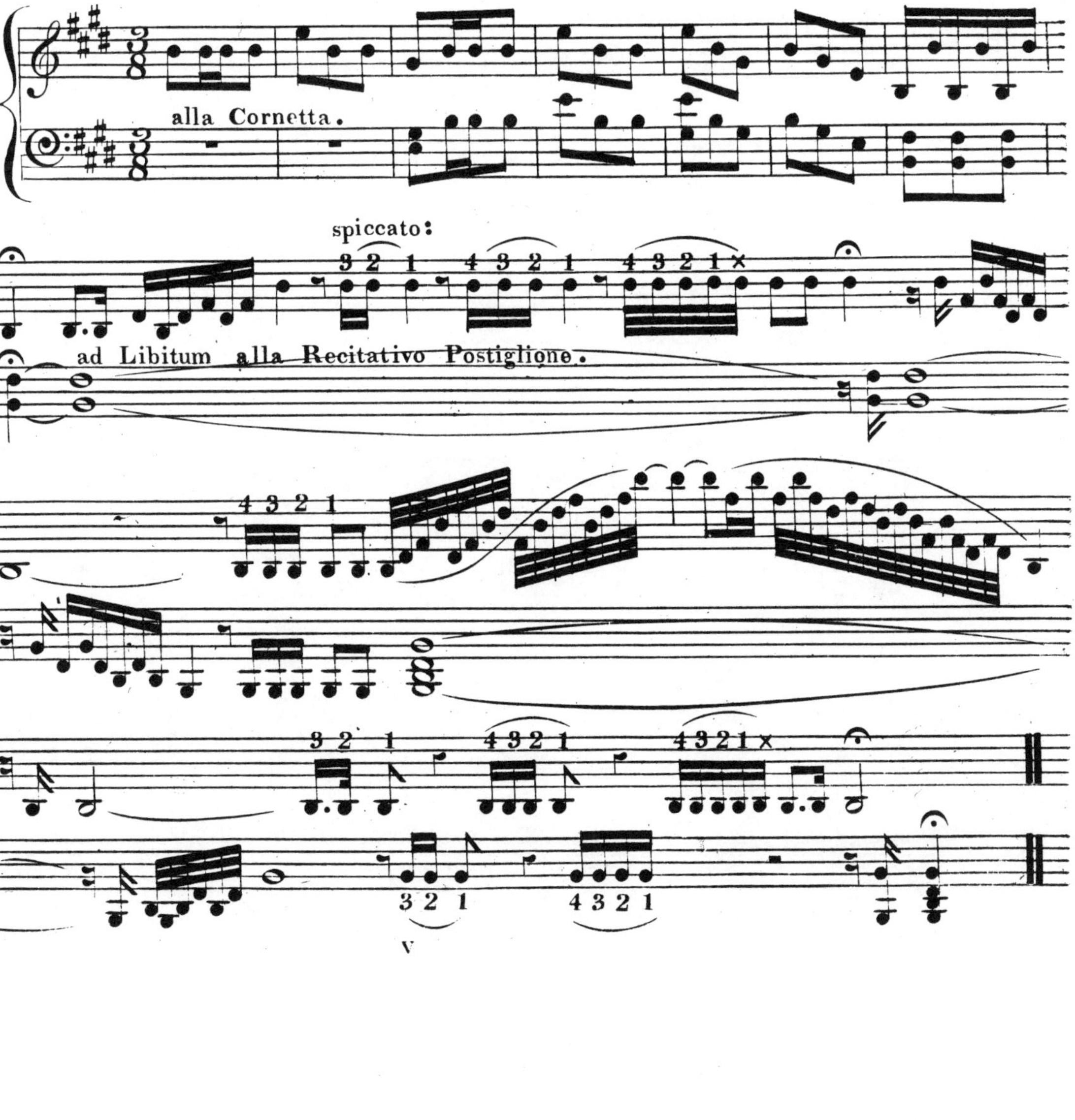
alla Cornetta.
spiccato:
ad Libitum alla Recitativo Postiglione.

Tempo Primo, cioe: con molto Animo.
Let others boast of London Town, It's Lords and Ladies, King and Crown! The
grandeur there is empty show, And vain the praise of high and low, Compar'd to
thee, whom all ap=prove, Fair Ci=ty of Fra=ter=nal Love! Compar'd to
thee, whom all ap=prove, Fair Ci=ty of Fra=ter=nal Love! "Phi
con Eufonia
la=del=phi=a!"
8 va
loco.

No scene or clime can charm like thee, (And I have
sail'd the world a = round,) For Beau=ty, Joy, and Friendship free, Thy Maids & Men are
far re = nown'd, Then bless the spot which all ap = prove, Fair Cit = y of Fra=
ter = nal Love, Fair Ci = = = = = = = = ty of Fra=ter=nal Love. = =

"Brotherly Love,"
"Brotherly
Love,
The maids who charm'd with love and song, The friends so true, so frank and

free All that I've known so oft, so long, Shall ev = er in my mem'=ry be, To
bless the spot which all ap=prove, Fair Ci = ty of Fra=ter = nal Love, Fair Cit = y
of Fra=ter = nal Love, Fair Ci = ty of Fra=ter=nal Love, = = = = = =
= = = = = = = "A = = mo = = = = = = = re."

MINORE.
And when I'm forc'd to bid fare=well, To all the charms that gain'd my heart, My hum=ble Muse on all shall dwell, And sing the praise thy joys im=part!
A PLACITO.
3 2 1
Tocca subito il Canto.

Tempo di Minuetto.
And when I'm forc'd to bid farewell, To all the charms that gain'd my heart, = = My
humble Muse, my humble Muse on all, on all shall dwell, And sing the praise thy
sempre crescendo.
joys impart, And sing the praise thy joys impart, And sing the praise thy joys, thy joys =
= = = im = = part, To bless the spot which all approve, To bless the spot, which
all ap = prove, Phi = = = = = = = la = del = phi = a

tr
senza rigore.
CODA, un poco piu animato alla Valso.
dolcemente.

cres = = = cen = = do.
8va:
loco:

3 2 1
3 2
1
3 2 1
3 2 1
rf Tardo:
Calando:

AVANCE et RETRAITE,

A MILITARY WALTZ FOR THE

Piano Forte,

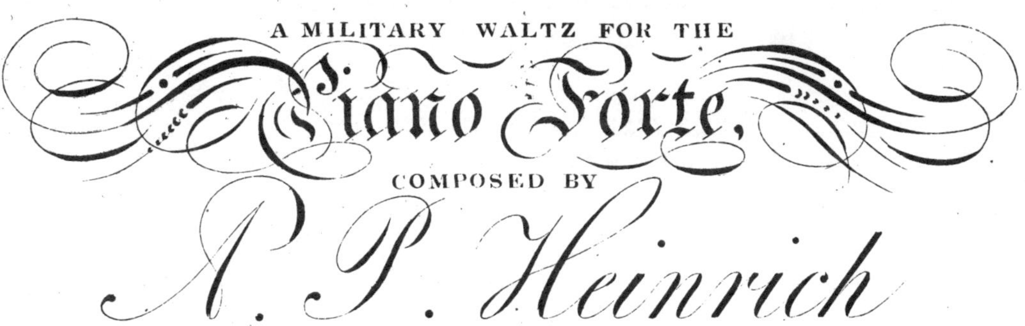

COMPOSED BY

A. P. Heinrich

 Pr:50.

Philadelphia, Published by BACON & HART, and by the AUTHOR, Kentucky.

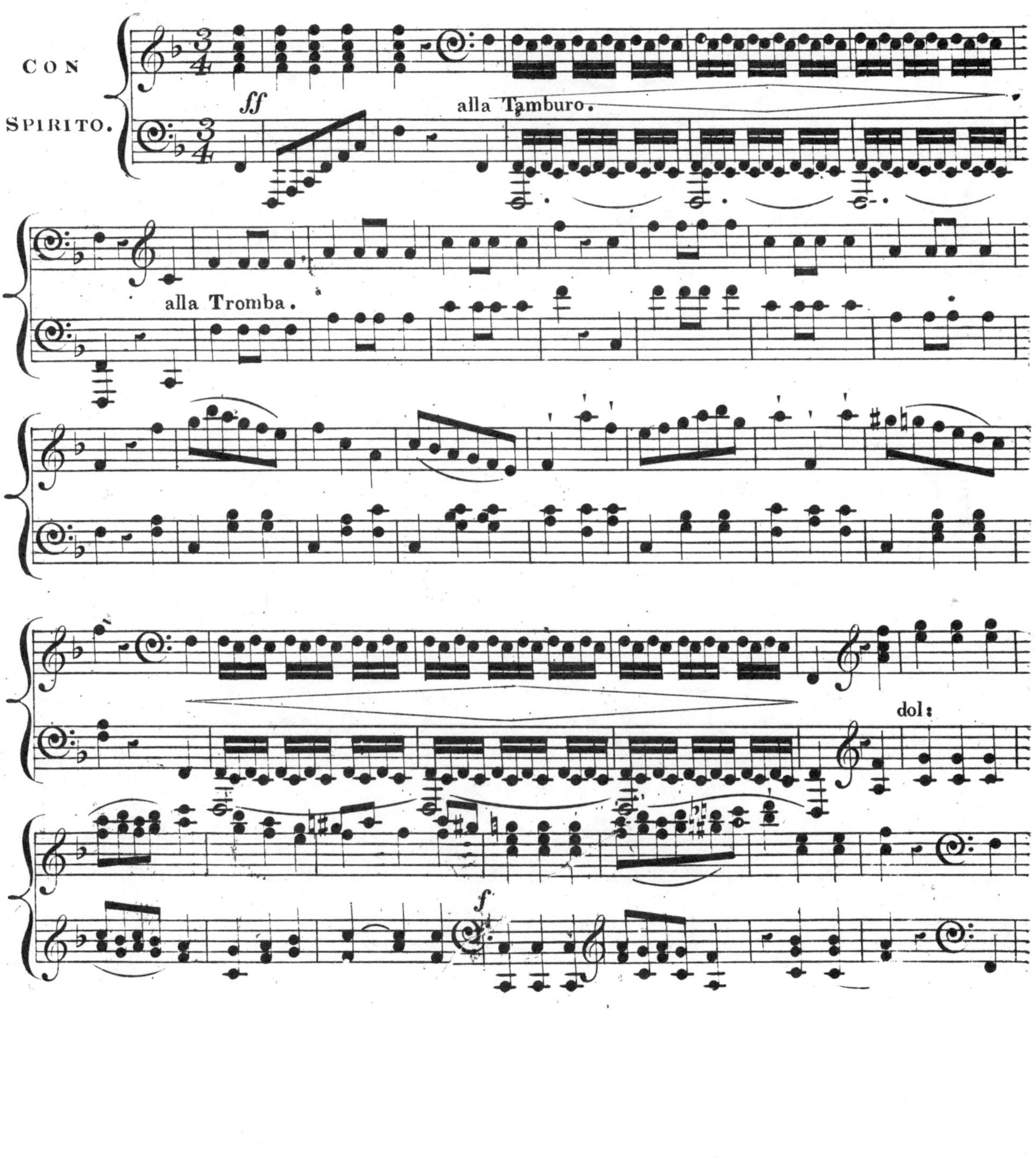
CON
SPIRITO.
ff
alla Tamburo.
alla Tromba.
dol:
f

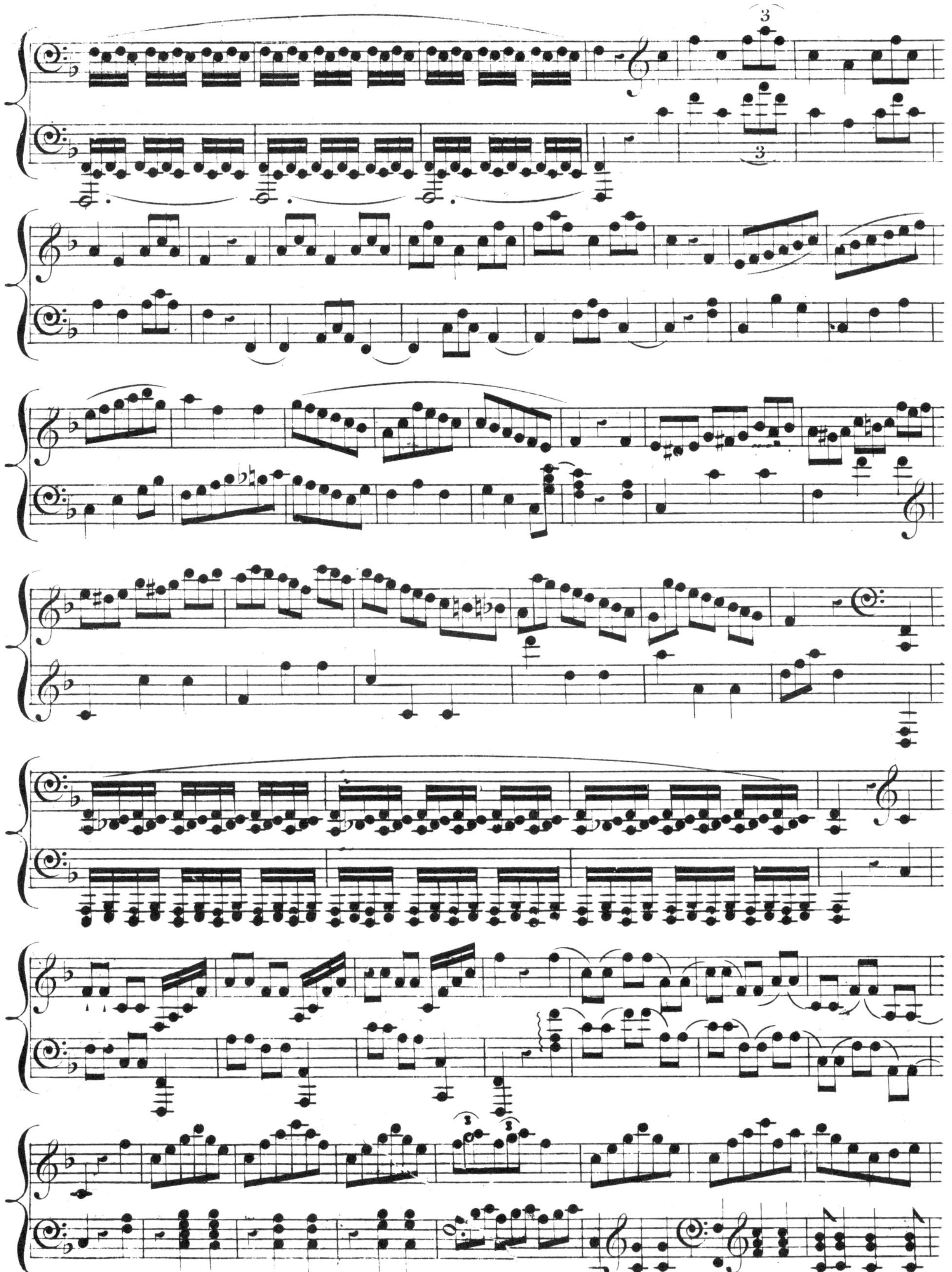
3
3

W

Magg e
Min e
Minore
Maggiore

8va piu alta
loco.
8va
Retro, or begin at the end, and end at the beginning.

VIOLIN,

WITH ACCOMPANIMENTS,

AND DEDICATED TO

Mess.rs C. F. & J. Hupfeld,

BY

A. P. HEINRICH.

Pr: 1.50

PHILADELPHIA, PUBLISHED BY BACON & HART, AND BY

THE AUTHOR, KENTUCKY.

X

TO MESS[RS] CHARLES F. AND JOHN HUPFELD,

DEAR SIRS,

The high admiration due to your musical talents, and the gratitude I owe to you, and family, for many instances of kindness, have chiefly prompted the present dedication. Having of late been led to make Music the subject of professional exercises, and the means of combating adversity, I thought I should also show to the Public, especially to the Heroes of the Bow, a small specimen of my own humble talents. There are many, among the principal Professors, and Amateurs of Music at Philadelphia &c. who have evinced marks of friendship towards me; and to the Inhabitants of Kentucky, (the State in which I now reside,) and other respectable Citizens of the United States, I acknowledge myself to be particularly indebted, for patronage: To them, and to you, these Compositions are now presented; and as they are the firstlings of my Muse, they may therefore be entitled to some indulgence; the more so, as they were drawn up in the wilds of America, where the minstrelsy of nature, the songsters of the air, next to other Virtuosos of the woods, have been my greatest inspirers of melody, harmony, and composition. Although of foreign growth, and reared as it were, in a musical country, where all are more or less conversant in such acquirements; yet have I, till recently, meditated so little on music, that I may justly call myself a Tyro in an art; which, tho' of so pleasing a nature, is very intricate in its principles, and execution, particularly on the Violin, the King of instruments, and the Pillar of the Orchestra. You, and the public perhaps will say, I rather should have used a tacet, or withheld a dedication: I acknowledge, that the modes of address, and the arts of pleasing, are a species of learning, that I have never yet acquired; but silence is not justifiable, when gratitude urges an acknowledgment; which feeling myself constrained to make, in some way; I thought the most natural course, at least for myself, was to turn the warm effusions of a grateful heart into music. Should my musical strains be well received, it will show, to whom I am indebted; but should a different fate await them, I can only assert, that the good motives I felt on the occasion, will soften the mortification of disappointment. It is not however, to my own feelings, but to the public judgment, and generosity that I appeal: I have therefore no further apology to offer; and will only add, that should these my humble efforts be made instrumental, either for practice, or amusement, I shall hereafter probably take courage to continue, with more aspiring publications: at the same time let it be remembered, that a well known Poet justly observes,

"Whoever thinks a faultless piece to see,
"Thinks what ne'er was, nor is, nor e'er shall be."

With such sentiments, I subscribe myself — Gentlemen,

Your highly obliged and
Very humble servant,

ANTHONY PHILIP HEINRICH.

TEMA DI MOZART.

GUSTOSO.
VAR: 3.
A
4
2
1
A
2
D
3
1
G
3
D
O
G
O
1
3
1
3
3
1
3
O
O
O
1
1
1
1
A
&
E
le doppie Corde si potrebbero sonare semplice o a piacere discreto.
VAR: 4.
RISOLUTO.
G
G
D
G
A
G
D
O
2
3
4
O
1
2
G
O
O
O
VAR: 5.
RADDOLCENDO.

CON MOLTO ESPRESSIONE.
VAR: 6.
ALLA POLACCA, l'accompagnamento pizzicato.
VAR: 7.
GRAZIOSO. e molto legato. Questa Variazione si potrebbe anche eseguire senza gli Posizioni marcate:
CON LEGGIADRIA.
VAR: 8.

X

ARPEGGIO.

VAR: 12.

Fine.

TEMA ORIGINALE.

TEMPO WALTZ.

VIOLINO PRIMO.

Grazioso.

BASSO.

il Basso sempre Da Capo.

VAR: 1.

VAR:2.
VAR:3.
VAR:4.

VAR: 5.
VAR: 6.
VAR: 7.

VAR: 8.
Poco più Presto.
ESTRO.
VAR: 9.
Tempo di Minuetto.
VAR: 10.
alla Trio.

Piu Animato.
VAR: 11.
VAR: 12.
Quasi Presto.
De A

VAR:13.
SEMPRE STACCATO. e sopra le Corde G e D.
VAR:14.
ff
D e A
a Gusto.
VAR:15.
&c
x

VAR: 16.
VAR: 17.

con Strepito.
VAR: 18.
legato
VAR: 19.
8va
DOLCEMENTE.
VAR: 20.
FINE.
D.C.

A CHROMATIC RAMBLE, OF THE PEREGRINE HARMONIST,

A. P. Heinrich.

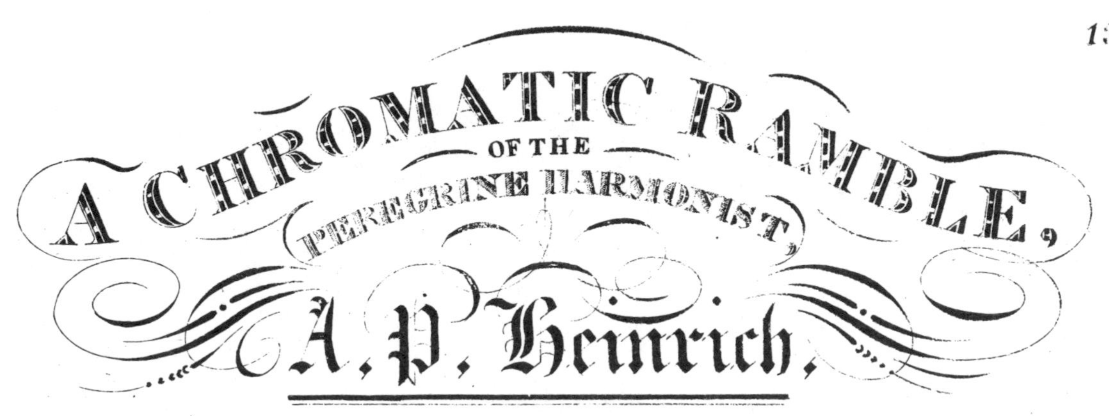

 Pr: 1,00.

Philadelphia, Published by BACON & HART, and by the AUTHOR, Kentucky.

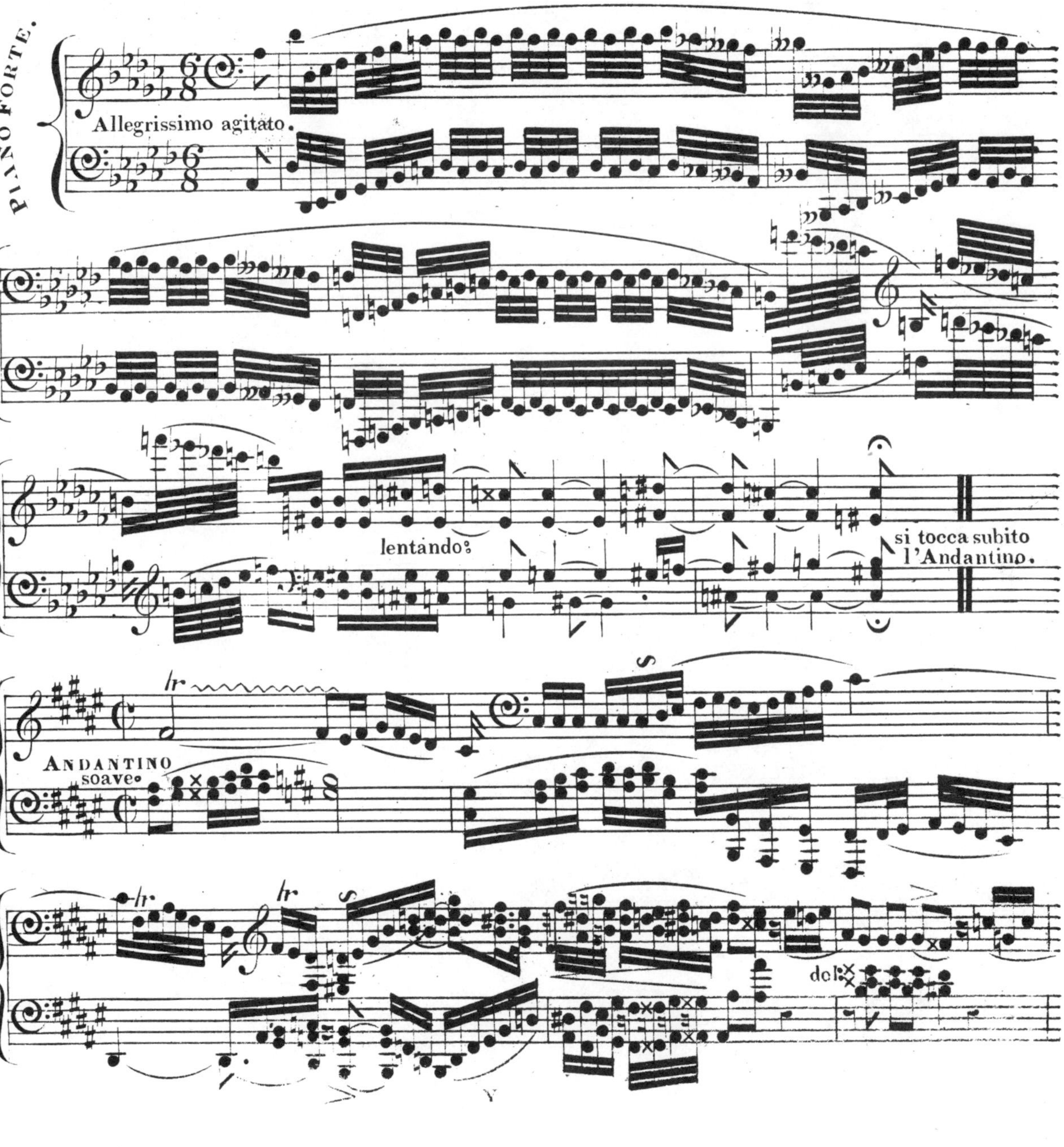
PIANO FORTE.
Allegrissimo agitato.
lentando.
si tocca subito l'Andantino.
ANDANTINO soave.
dol:

AD LIB:
espress:
Allegro assai e sempre espressivo.
IL CANTO.
A = mong the flats the flats
and sharps and sharps a te = = = = = = = = = = =
legato.
= = = dious jour = = = = = = = = = = = ney trav = el
Il Piano Forte molto legato.
And lo =

= = = = = = se yourself in knots in 8kno = = = = = = = = = = = = = = =
= ts of Chords Chords Chords of Chords of Chords of Chords And
then those knots un = rav = el And then those knots un = rav = el those
kno = = = = = = = = = = = = = ts un = rav = el Then sigh
and die and faint in bli = = = = = =
V.S.

ss ex = tat = ic ex = tat = ic ex = tat = ic
And then the half tones try
espress.
the half tones the half tones the
half = = = = = = = = = = = = = = = tones For a touch of
the chro = mat = ic for a touch of the chromatic a touth = =
= = = = = = = = a touch of the chroma = = = = = = = =

tic For a touch For a touch For a
touch For a touch of the chroma tic
Chro ma tic Then where you set
out come a=gain Then where you set out come a=gain And
now you're welcome and now you're welcome ho
sempre Accelerando.

6
tr
me a
a=gain a=gain a=gain a gain a=gain a=gain "A
gain
Ad Lib:
Ca
tr
sa."
ALLEGRO DI MOLTO.
sf

sempre legato.
sempre accelerando e crescendo
ff Presto.
Adagio.
Ad Lib:
8va Alt:
si continua subito.

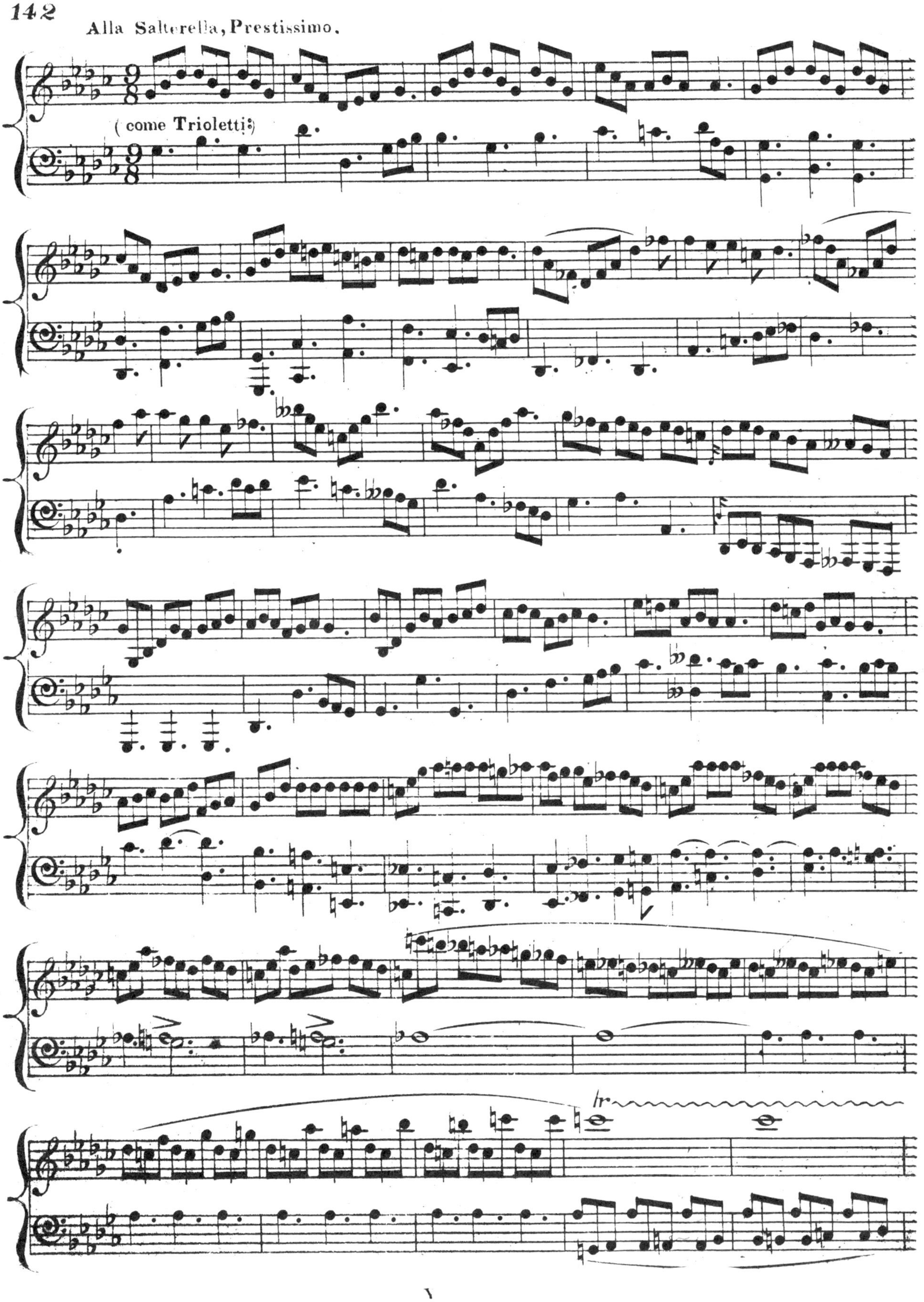
Alla Salterella, Prestissimo.
(come Trioletti)

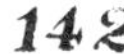

L'istesso tempo, cioè velocissimo:
Furibondo.
dol:
8 va: alt.
Sempre Crescendo.
loco:

5
tr
5

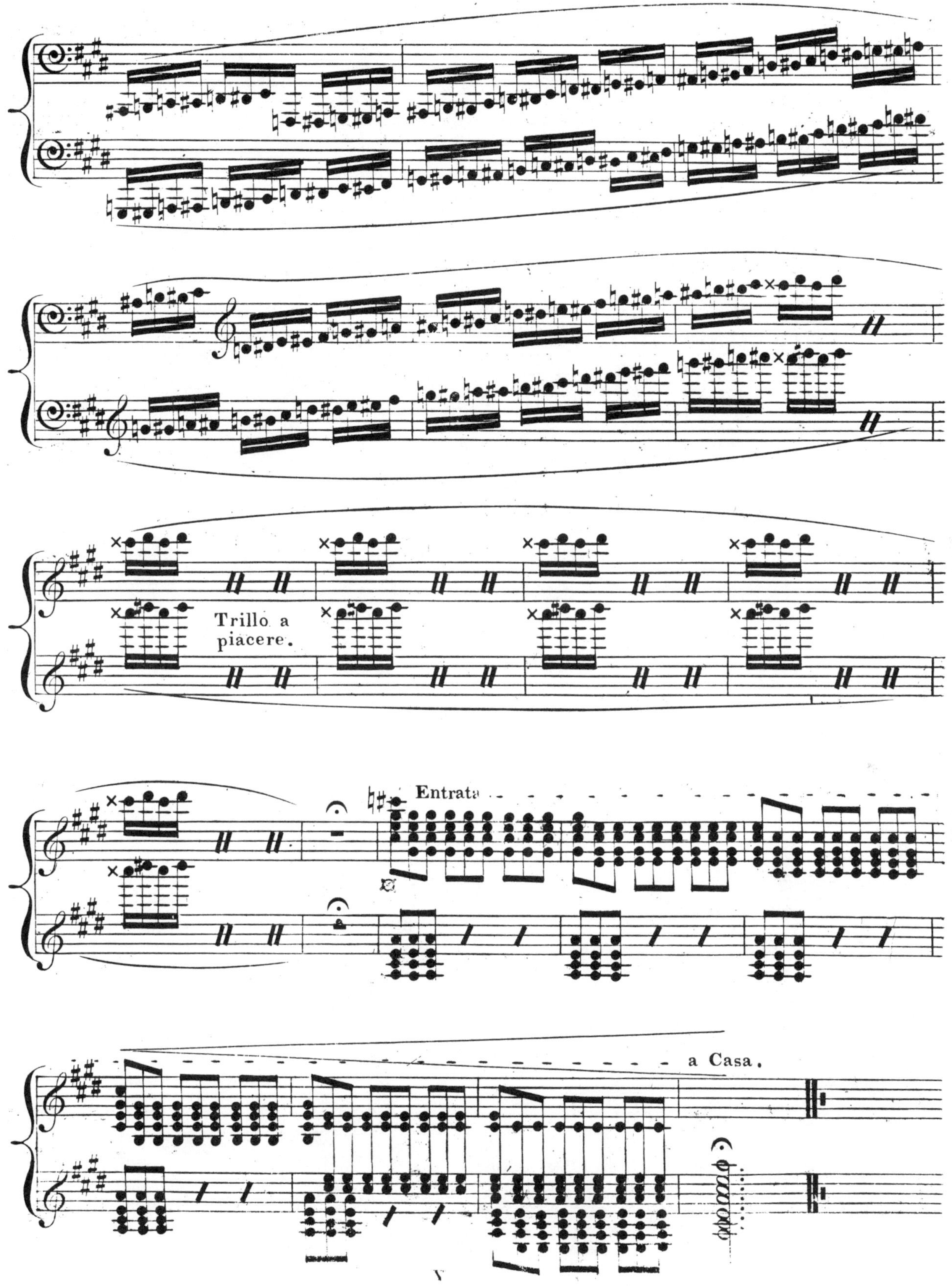
Trillo a piacere.
Entrata
a Casa.

CODA.

Andantino
Animato.
spiccato.
My Harp a=wake! a=wake a=gain, O! strike the
soul in=spiring string, No more in pen = sive notes com=plain, But waft to
gra= = titude the strain, No more in pensive notes com=plain, But wa= =
= ft to gratitude the strain, And "Alma Ma= = = =ters" off'ring bring. And
"Al= = ma Maters" off'ring bring.
8va
loco:

2

Ye Friends most dear! this heart would pay
The grateful meed to kindness due;
And when afar that heart shall stray,
The wanderer — urged by fate away —
His song of love shall wake to you.

3

A sylvan Muse inspires his theme
Yet kindly, Hope his bosom cheers,
That ye who bask in fancy's dream,
By Pleasure wafted down the stream,
May not disdain the child of tears.

4

Ye generous Patrons of the Muse,
May halcyon peace on you attend;
While smiling Love, the floweret strews,
May bland contentment ne'er refuse,
To crown with bliss the minstrel's FRIEND.

Note. The Author takes this opportunity to acknowledge his obligation to his Poetical Friend Mr. Wm. B. Tappan for the preceding Stanzas.

SUPPLEMENT.

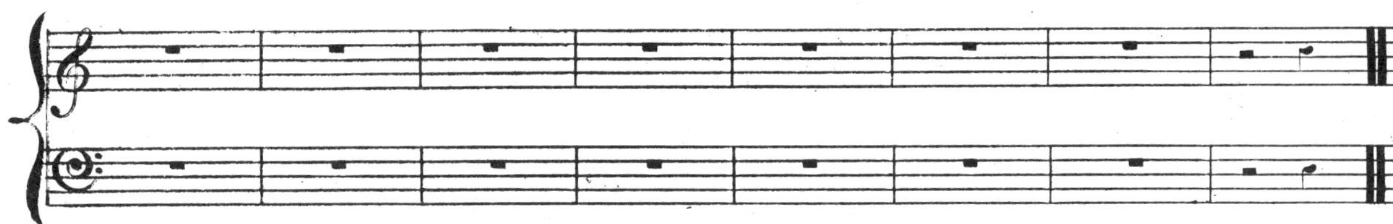

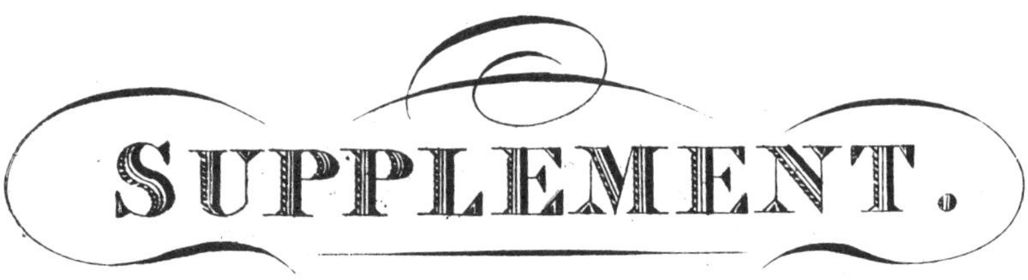

To my Virtuoso Friends.___ A. P. Heinrich.

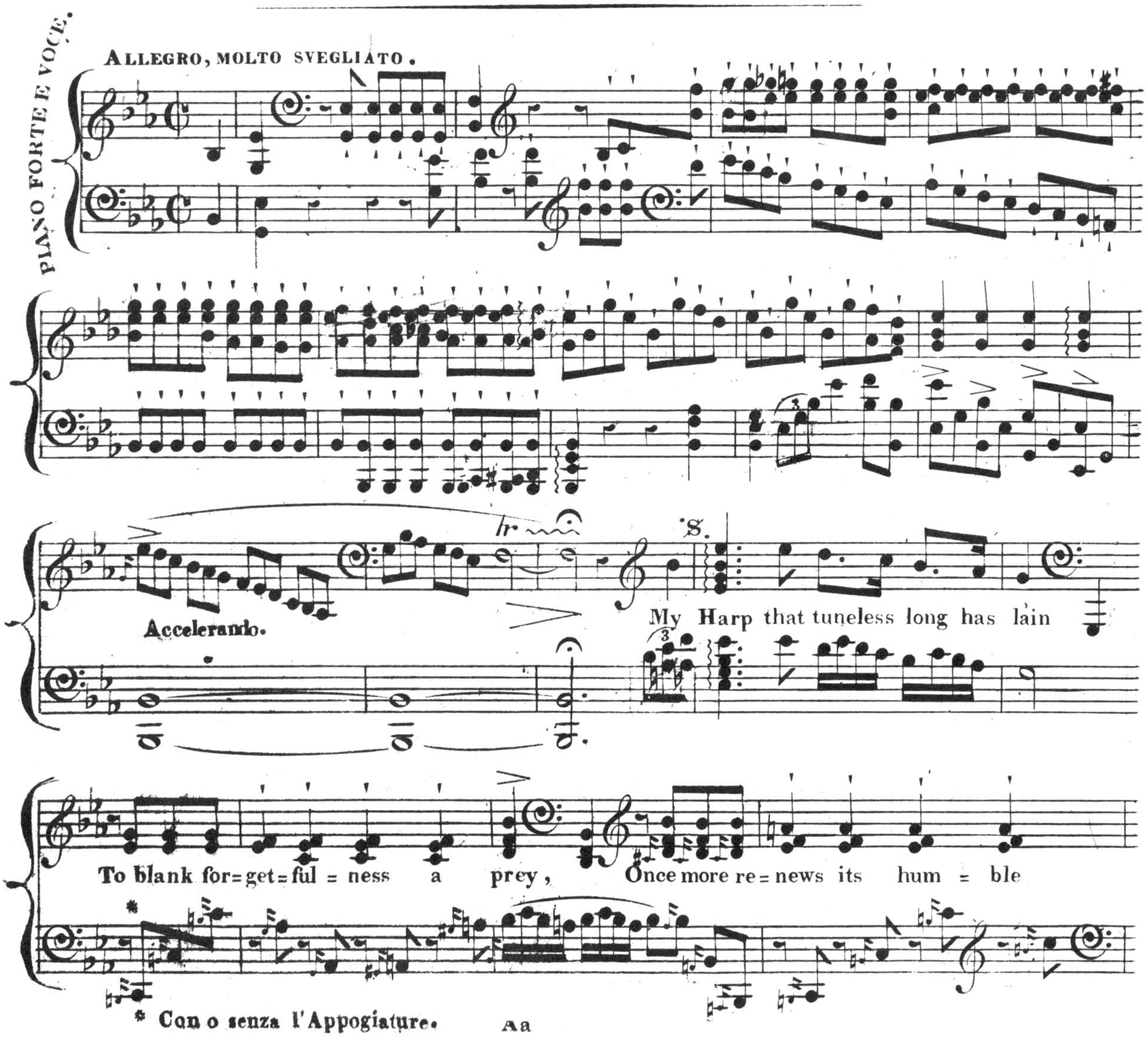

PIANO FORTE E VOCE.
ALLEGRO, MOLTO SVEGLIATO.
Accelerando.
tr
8.
My Harp that tuneless long has lain
To blank for=get=ful = ness a prey,
Once more re=news its hum = ble

* Con o senza l'Appogiature.

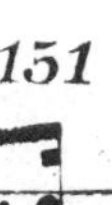

strain Not for ap = plause or smiles to gain But to its

a tempo.

frie = = = = = = = = = = = nds a tri = bute pay = = = Ye friends be =

espr: discreto. dol:

= lov'd, ye cho = sen few Whose kindness claims my thanks sincere May Heav'n your paths with

ro = ses strew Nor pain or sorrow may you know How long or short you wan = der

here How long or short you wander here How long or short you wan =

= = = = = = = = = = = = = = = der here.

3

May plenty ope her silver horn,
And strew its treasures at your feet
And may on gentle breezes borne,
Arise at eve and early morn,
The song of GRATITUDE most sweet

4

May all the blessings heaven bestows,
On you like evening dew decend;
And when the stream of sorrow flows,
To calm your grief, and sooth your woes,
O may you never want a FRIEND.

Note — The Poetry selected from the Works of the Boston Bard.

"The Sons of the Woods,"

AN INDIAN WAR-SONG

WRITTEN BY H. C. Lewis, COMPOSED BY

A. P. HEINRICH.

 Pr: 38.

Philadelphia, Published by BACON & HART, and by the AUTHOR, Kentucky.

PRESTISSIMO FURIOSO.

un poco piu commodo, ma con gran Forza.

War-whoop.

accelerando.

ff

Tocca subito il Canto.

CANTO.
See! see! on yonder redd'ning sky, The blaze of war ascending high;
FURIBONDO.
Sons of the Woods, now quick pre = pare For war and spoil — our foes are
near! For war and spoil — our foes are near! our foes are near!
Our silent march shall find the foe, Our deadly rifles lay him

low, Our toma = hawks con = firm the blow, And scalping knives the vict'ry
show. = = = = = = = = = =
CHORUS.
Our - silent march shall find the
foe, Our deadly rifles lay him low, Our tom = a = hawks con = firm the
blow, And scalping knives the vict'= ry show.
ff

2

Hark! hark! the war whoop! quick, advance,
Blaze high the fires, begin the dance,
Awake the song — the song of war,
The bugles sound, now march afar.

Upon the shore we'll meet the foe,
Or in our woods deal hard the blow;
In summer's heat, or winter's snow,
O'er hill and dale, his blood shall flow.

CHORUS — Our silent march, &c.

3

Sons of the Woods, come, no delay,
Farewell, our wives! Now, now away,
To meet th'invaders of our shore,
And lay them lifeless in their gore.

We'll drive the flying o'er the plain,
To seek once more the briny main;
Our woods we'll strew with thousands slain,
And with their blood the herbage stain.

CHORUS — Our silent march, &c.

4

No tender thoughts of home or wife,
Shall now unnerve the arm of strife;
Till all is victory, to return,
No wish within the heart shall burn.

Till far away is every foe,
Peace shall no more our bosoms know;
Nor shall, till Justice stays the blow,
The tomahawk be buried low.

CHORUS — Our silent march, &c.

Marcia di Ballo,

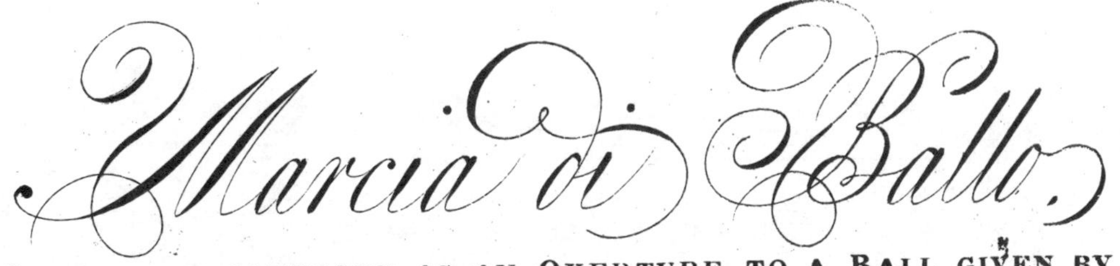

ORIGINALLY COMPOSED AS AN OVERTURE TO A BALL GIVEN BY

MAJOR SMILEY,

OF BARDSTOWN, KENTUCKY,

AND NOW ARRANGED FOR THE **Piano Forte** BY ITS AUTHOR,

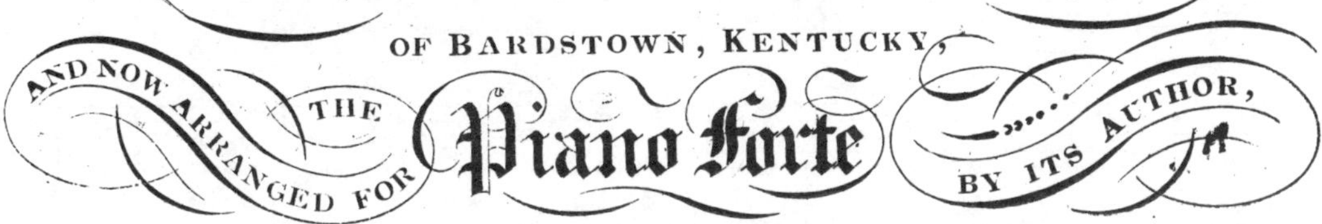

A. P. HEINRICH.

 Pr: 75.

Philadelphia, Published by BACON & HART, and by the AUTHOR, Kentucky.

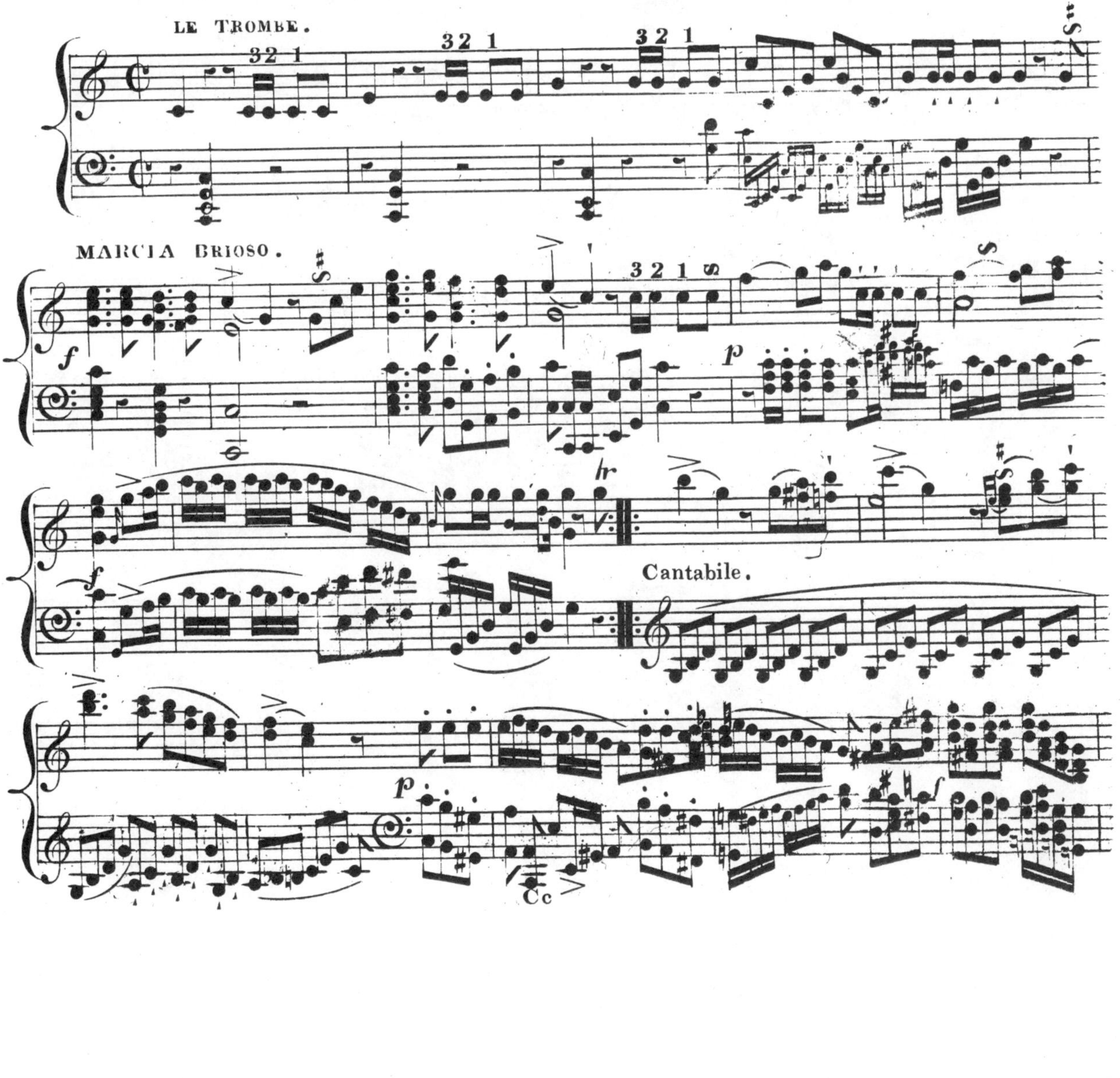
LE TROMBE.
3 2 1
MARCIA BRIOSO.
f
p
Cantabile.
Cc

espress:
1mo
2do
TRIO.
8va
loco.
1mo.
2do.
MINORE.
dol:
Legato.
8va.

* Since I[st] Edition, forming part of the Allegro movement, in the Overture of the 'CHILD of the MOUNTAIN,' &c.

p
p
espress:
espress:

cres:
ff
CODA.
YANKEE DOODLE.
p
V.S.

p
cres:
p
8va
loco.
8va
loco.
pp
f
rf
ff

8va
loco:
bis:
2d
Cc

 Pr: 25.

Philadelphia Published by BACON & HART, and by the AUTHOR Kentucky.

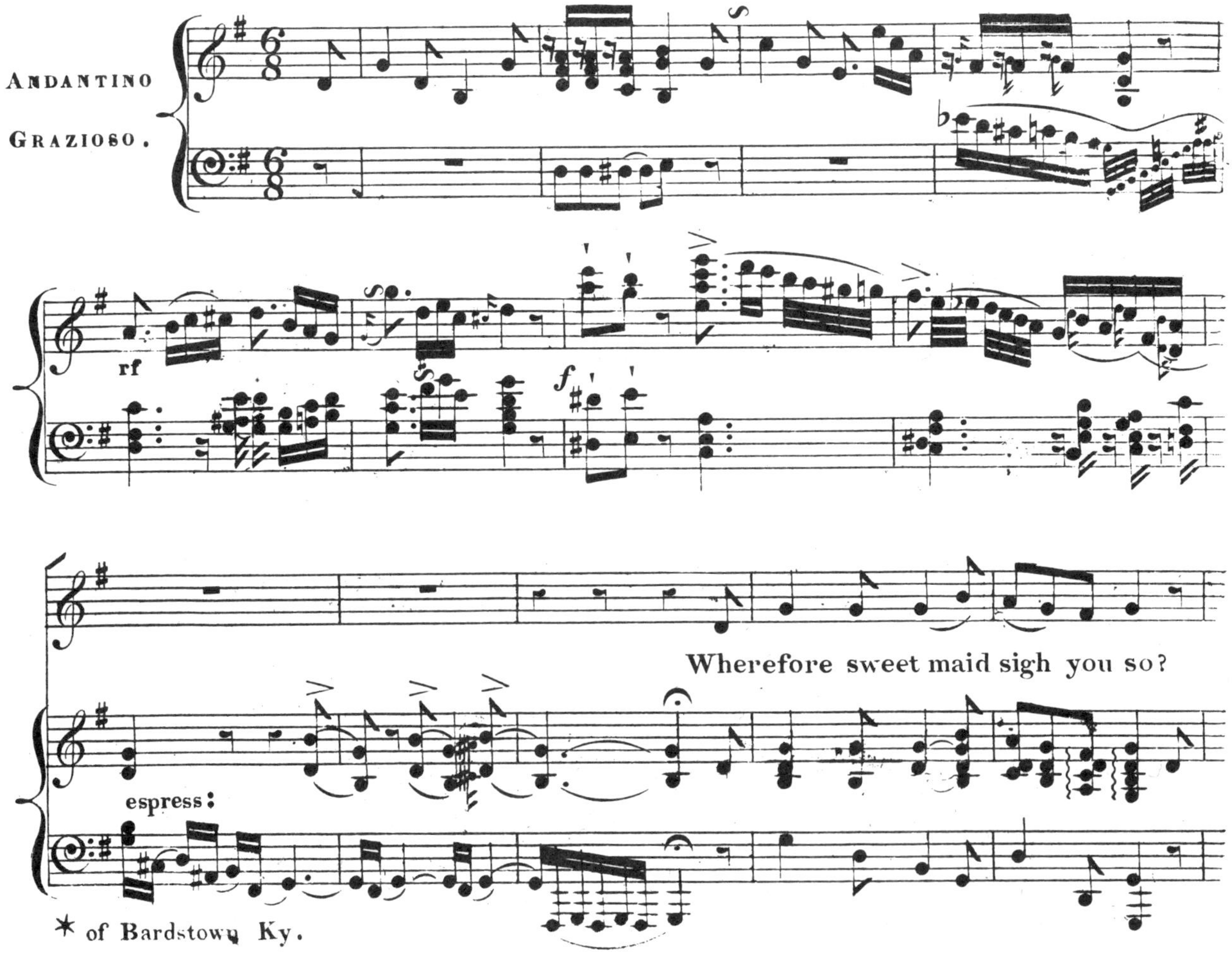

ANDANTINO GRAZIOSO.

rf

f

espress:

Wherefore sweet maid sigh you so?

* of Bardstown Ky.

2

O What has he for whom you sigh,
That is not also mine;
A breast on which you softly lie,
And a heart, but that is thine.

3

Therefore sweet maid, sigh not so,
Nor let your soft cheek fade;
Prithee! then love no more for woe,
But love for joy, sweet Maid!

THREE COTILLIONS,

COMPOSED AND ARRANGED FOR THE PIANO FORTE BY

A.P.HEINRICH.

Philadelphia, Published by BACON & HART, and by the AUTHOR, Kentucky. Pr:25.

LUCIADE.

* Introduced in to the Melo Drama of the CHILD of the MOUNTAIN, and danced by Miss K Ee. DURANG.

Tutti:
dolː
Flauti.
f
Fine.
Violino solo.
Flauto solo.
MINORE. Solo Violino.
Da Capo:
Solo Violino.
Tutti.
da Capo.

A DIVERTIMENTO FOR THE Piano Forte

COMPOSED, AND RESPECTFULLY DEDICATED TO

Mrs. John Speed

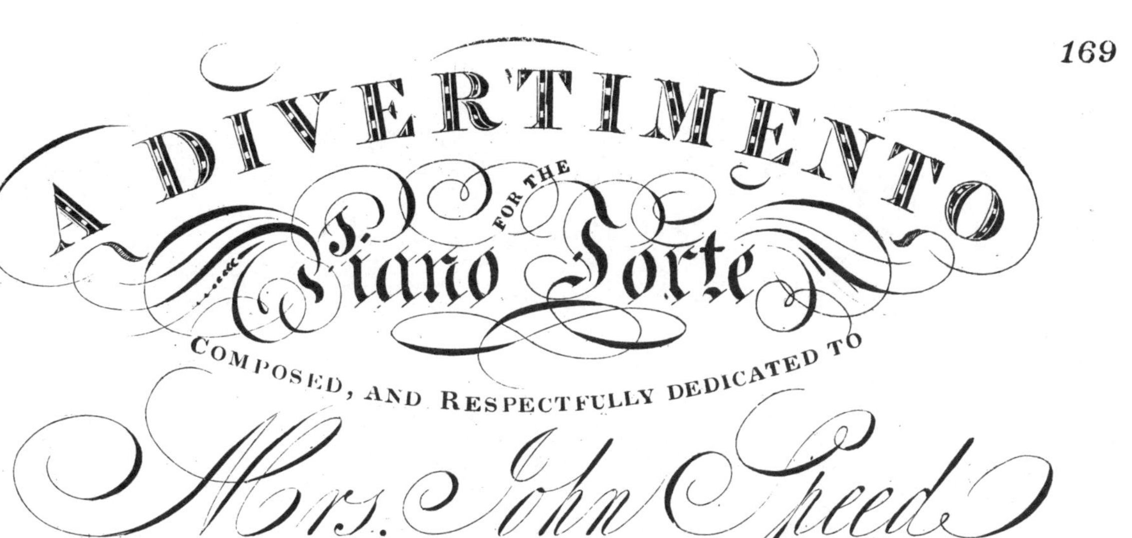

OF FARMINGTON, KY. BY

A. P. HEINRICH.

 Pr: 50.

Philadelphia Published by BACON & HART and by the AUTHOR Kentucky.

FARMINGTON MINUET.

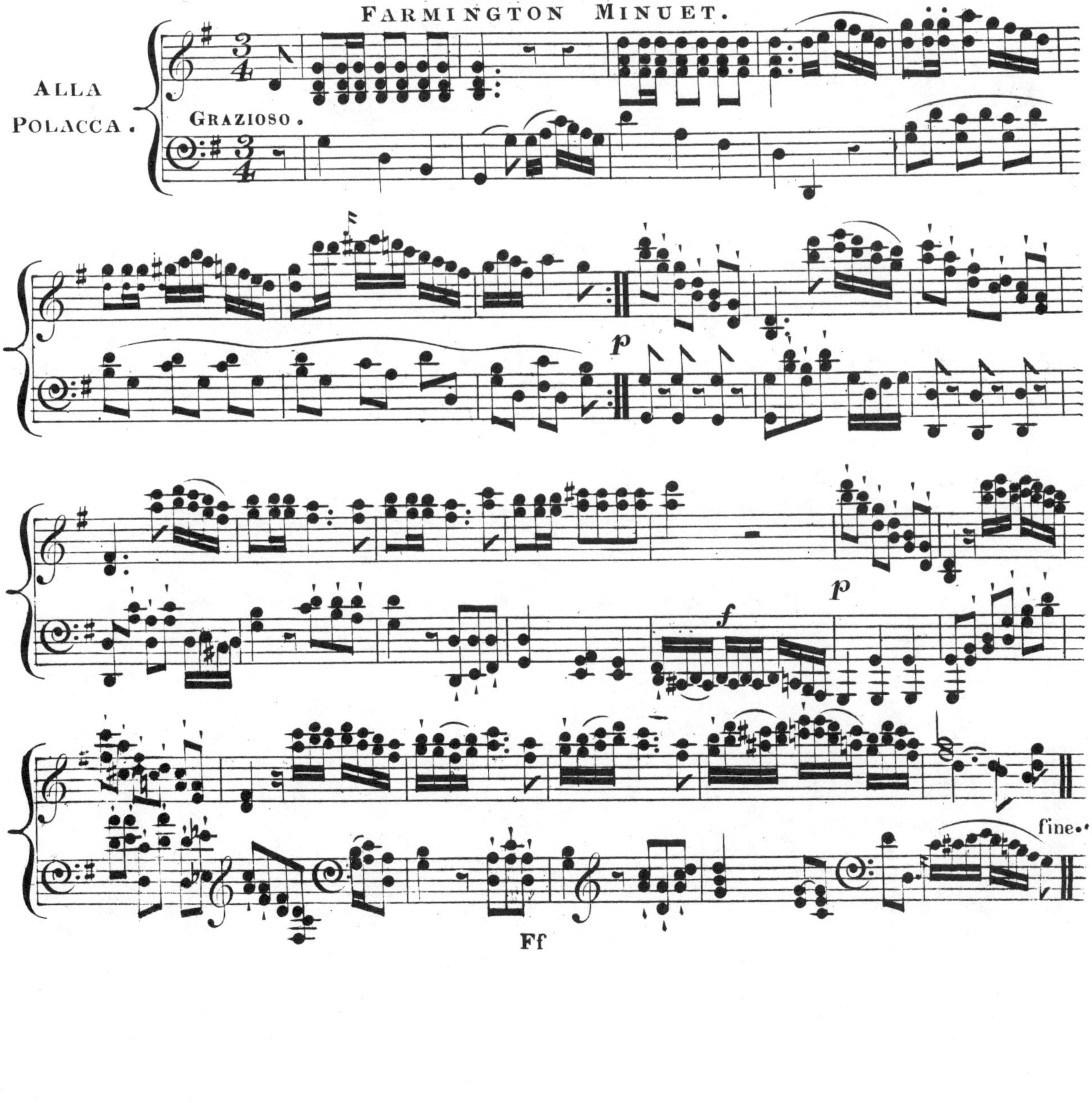
ALLA POLACCA.
GRAZIOSO.
p
f
p
fine.

TRIO MINORE.
MINUET DA CAPO.
FARMINGTON ALLEMANDE.
MODERATO.

Coda, Piu vivo, quasi Presto.
sf
tr

FARMINGTON MARCH.

CON BRIO.

Ben Marcato.

1st

2d

3 2 1
espress:
TRIO. Cantabile.
Fine.
f
p
f
dol:
March da Capo.

A SONG WRITTEN BY

ROBERT BURNS,

COMPOSED AND DEDICATED TO

BY

A. P. HEINRICH.

 Pr: 50.

Philadelphia, Published by BACON & HART, and by the AUTHOR, Kentucky.

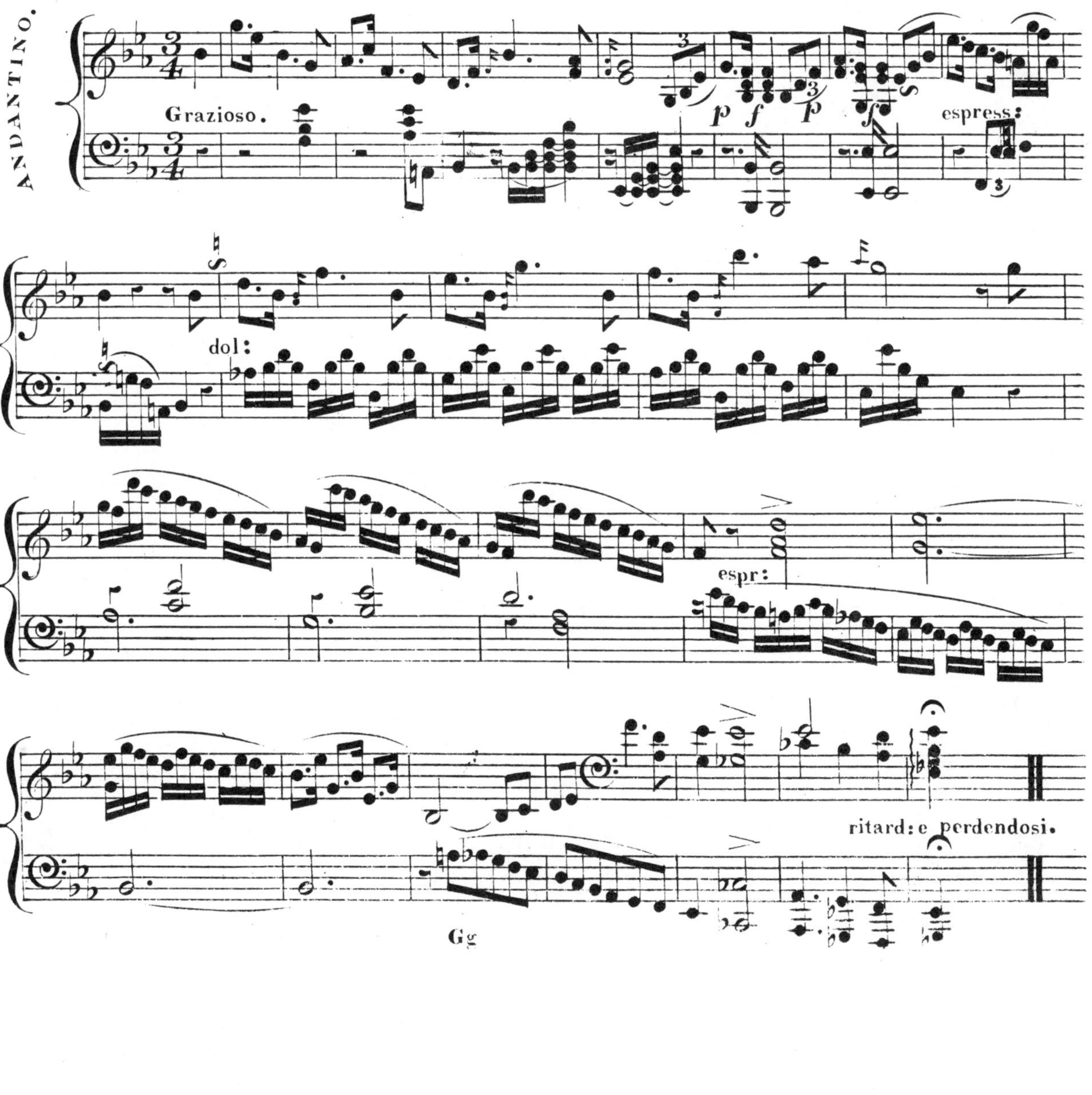

ANDANTINO.

Grazioso. p f p f espress:

dol:

espr:

ritard: e perdendosi.

From thee E = li = za, I must go, And from my na = = = tive shore;
The cruel fates be = tween us throw, A
boundless Ocean's roar.
espress:
But boundless Oceans roar = ing wide, Be = tween my Love and

me; They nev = er, nev = = = er can divide, My heart and soul from thee, my heart and

soul from thee.

dol:

espress.

Farewell! farewell E = li = za dear! The maid that I a = dore;

A boding voice is
in my ear We part to meet no more
dol:
f
But the
last throb that leaves my heart my heart While Death stands vic = tor by _ _ That
p con molto espress.
throb E = liza is thy part And thine that la = = = = = test sigh that la = = test
affetuoso.
espress.
poco ad lib:

sigh
sospirando:
colla voce.
espress:
graz:
rf
ritard: e perdendosi.

Farewell to Farmington!

A COTILLION, ARRANGED FOR THE PIANO FORTE.

BY THE AUTHOR, A. P. HEINRICH.

 Pr. 12.

Philadelphia, Published by BACON & Co, and by the AUTHOR, Kentucky.

SAY WHAT IS THAT HEART!

SONG, WRITTEN BY

Peter W. Grayson Esq.

COMPOSED BY

A. P. Heinrich.

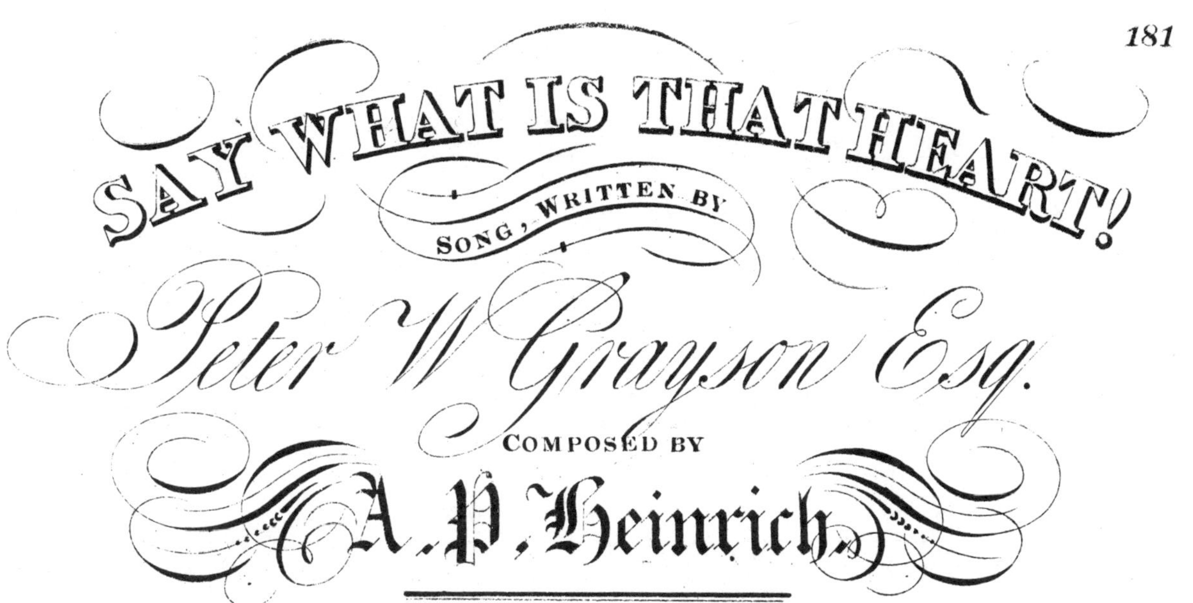

 Pr: 62.

Philadelphia, Published by BACON & HART, and by the AUTHOR, Kentucky.

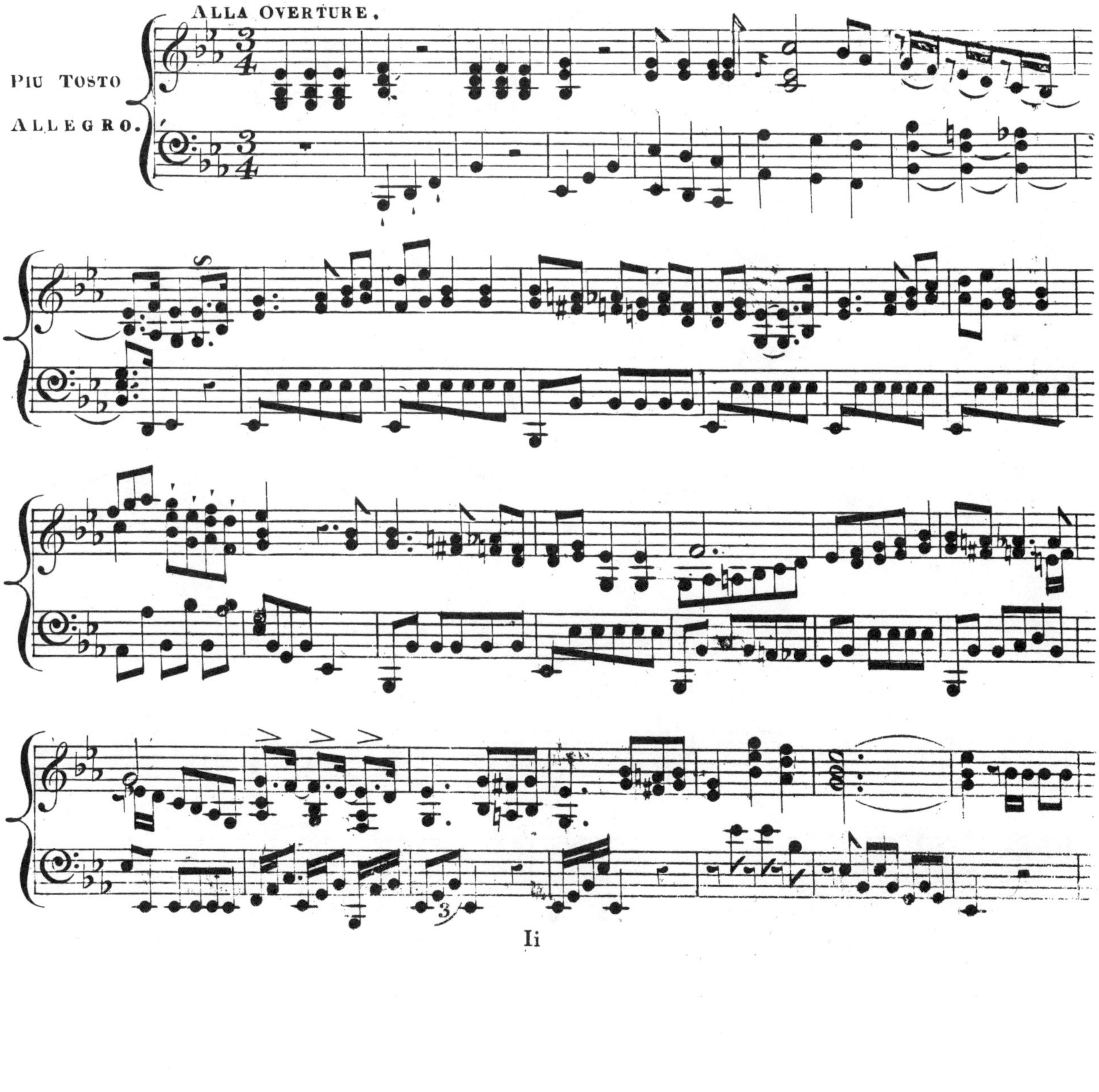

ALLA OVERTURE.
PIU TOSTO
ALLEGRO.

Say, what is that heart that can promise its faith And its love all to one till it
withers in death, That at noon can for= get the warm vows of the morn, And at
evening, O strange! be freezing with scorn.
That in moments of rapture when Fortune does shine, Will

smile o'er its object and call it di = vine; That in mo = ments of rap = ture when
For = tune does shine, Will smile o'er its ob = ject and call it di = vine; And
when clouds gather o'er will leave it to die, With a sneer of the lip, And the
scowl of an eye.

And yet is not
that one of feel = ing more strange,_ _ Whose love _ _ leaves an object that
8va._ _ _ _ _ _ _ loco:
nothing can change; All tired and sated as the rose finds its doom, In the

ve = = ry same sunshine that gave it its bloom.
They are clouds in the sky, as false as they're
bright; Form'd but for one minute to live in the light, They are clouds in the
sky, as false as they're bright, Form'd but for one minute to live in the

light, Whose bright fairy hues are changing for = ever, Then such could I take to my
8va
loco:
bo = som? O never!
ad lib.
a Tempo.
a tempo:
rit:
p
f

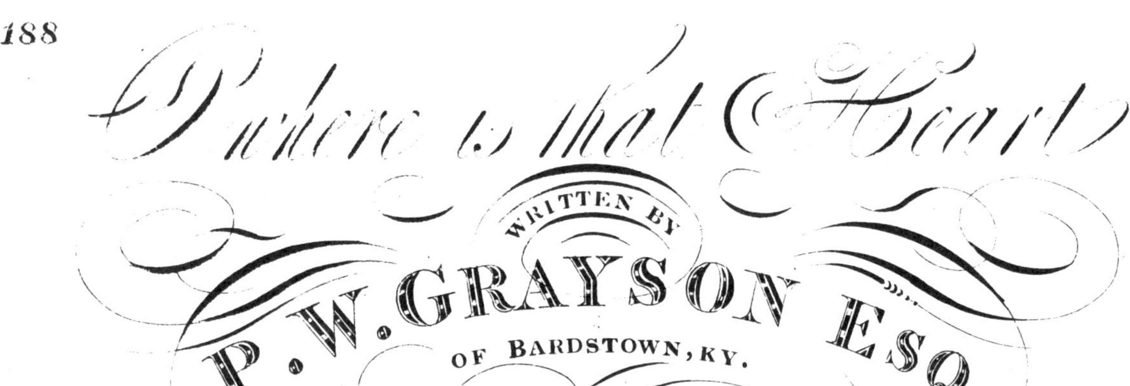

O where is that Heart

WRITTEN BY
P. W. GRAYSON ESQ.
OF BARDSTOWN, KY.
COMPOSED BY
A. P. HEINRICH.

 Pr:25.

Philadelphia, Published by BACON & HART, and by the Author, Kentucky.

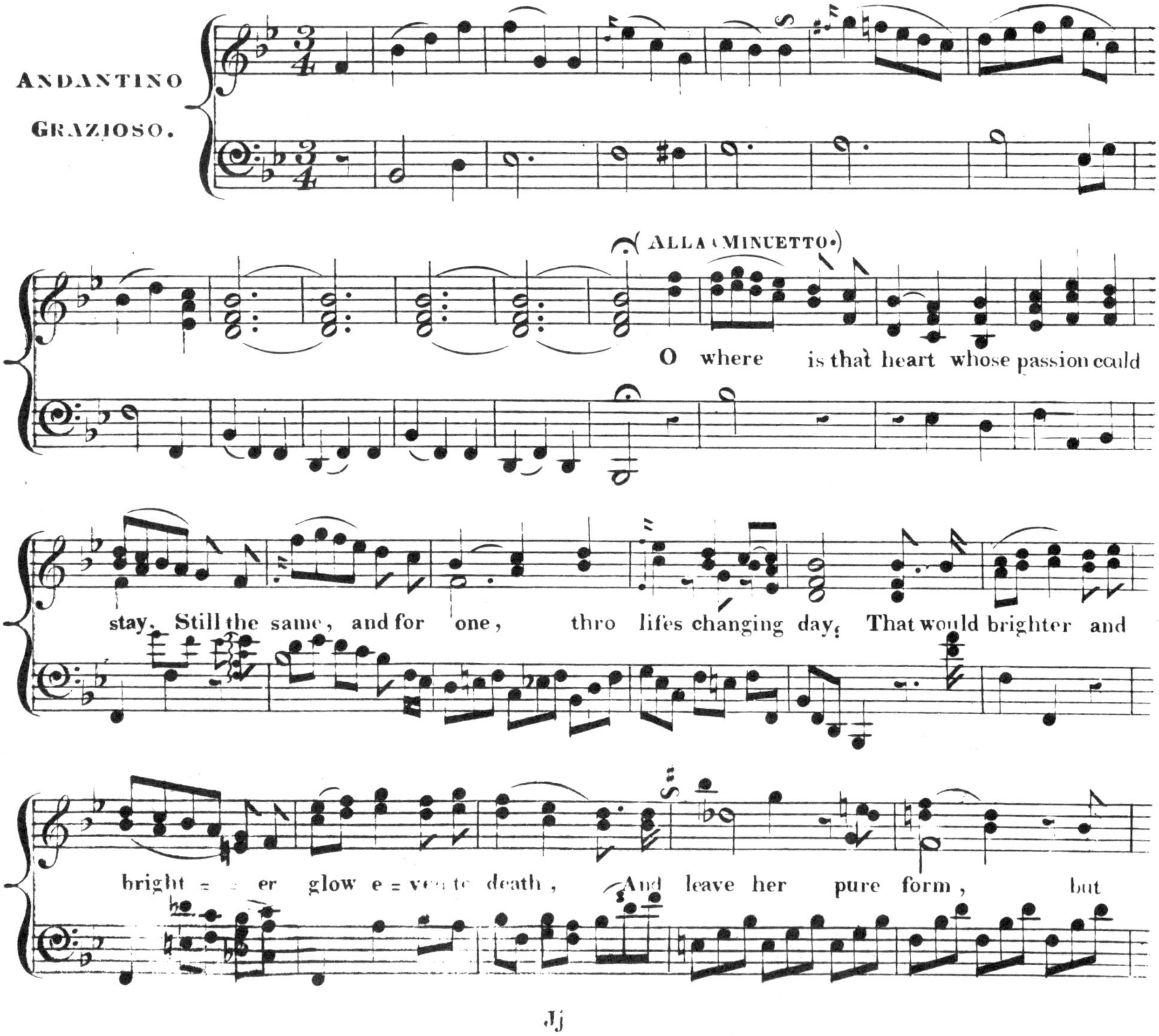
ANDANTINO GRAZIOSO.
(ALLA MINUETTO.)
O where is that heart whose passion could
stay. Still the same, and for one, thro lifes changing day;
That would brighter and bright = er glow e = ven to death,
And leave her pure form, but

2

That when Fortune is kind, in shade hides her zeal,
For the balm of her love hath no wound to heal;
But when sorrows come on and cloud all the scene,
With the light of her smile brings Hope back again.

3

'Tis a star in the sky that but faintly gleams,
While the sun on the earth pours the bliss of his beams;
But when darkness and clouds, come on with the night,
Shines forth in her beauty, all tearful and bright.

FROM "SONGS OF JUDAH" BY

COMPOSED AND DEDICATED TO

Mrs Sarah Ward Grayson,

OF LOUISVILLE, KY. BY

A. P. HEINRICH.

 Pr: 25.

Philadelphia Published by BACON & HART and by the AUTHOR Kentucky.

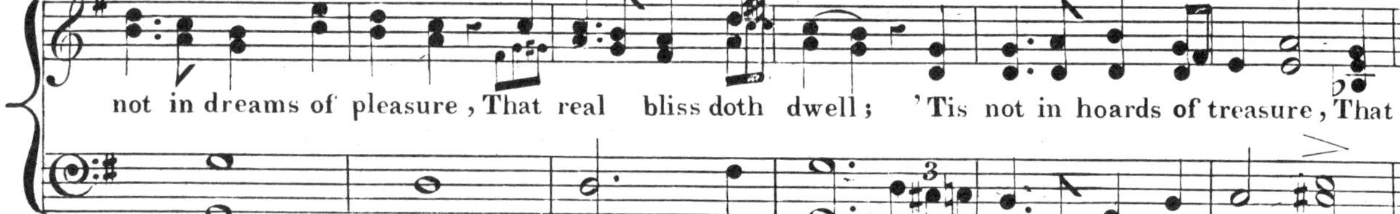

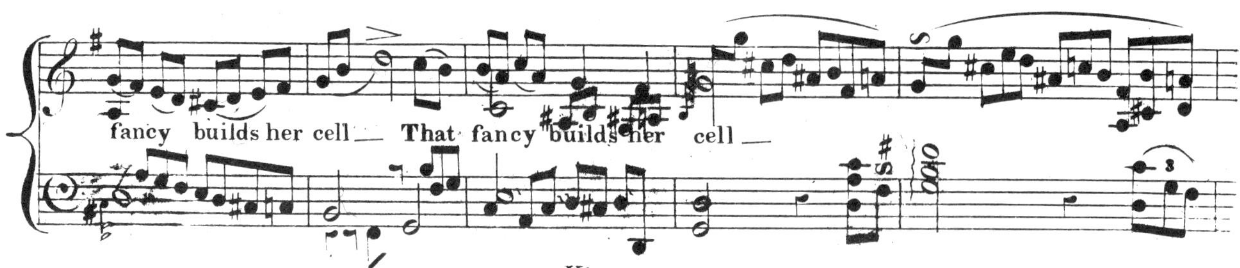

3

Delight sincere reposes,
And beams from beauty's eye;
More sweet than summer roses,
Is beauty's nectared sigh!

4

Then may each true endeavour,
With beauty's smile be blest;
Affection pillow ever
On Woman's faithful breast.

Note: The Author percieves that he has inadvertently copied a few bars Melody from Mozart.

THE SARAH.

A COTILLION, COMPOSED BY A. P. HEINRICH.

 Pr: 25.

Philadelphia, Published by BACON & HART, and by the AUTHOR, Kentucky.

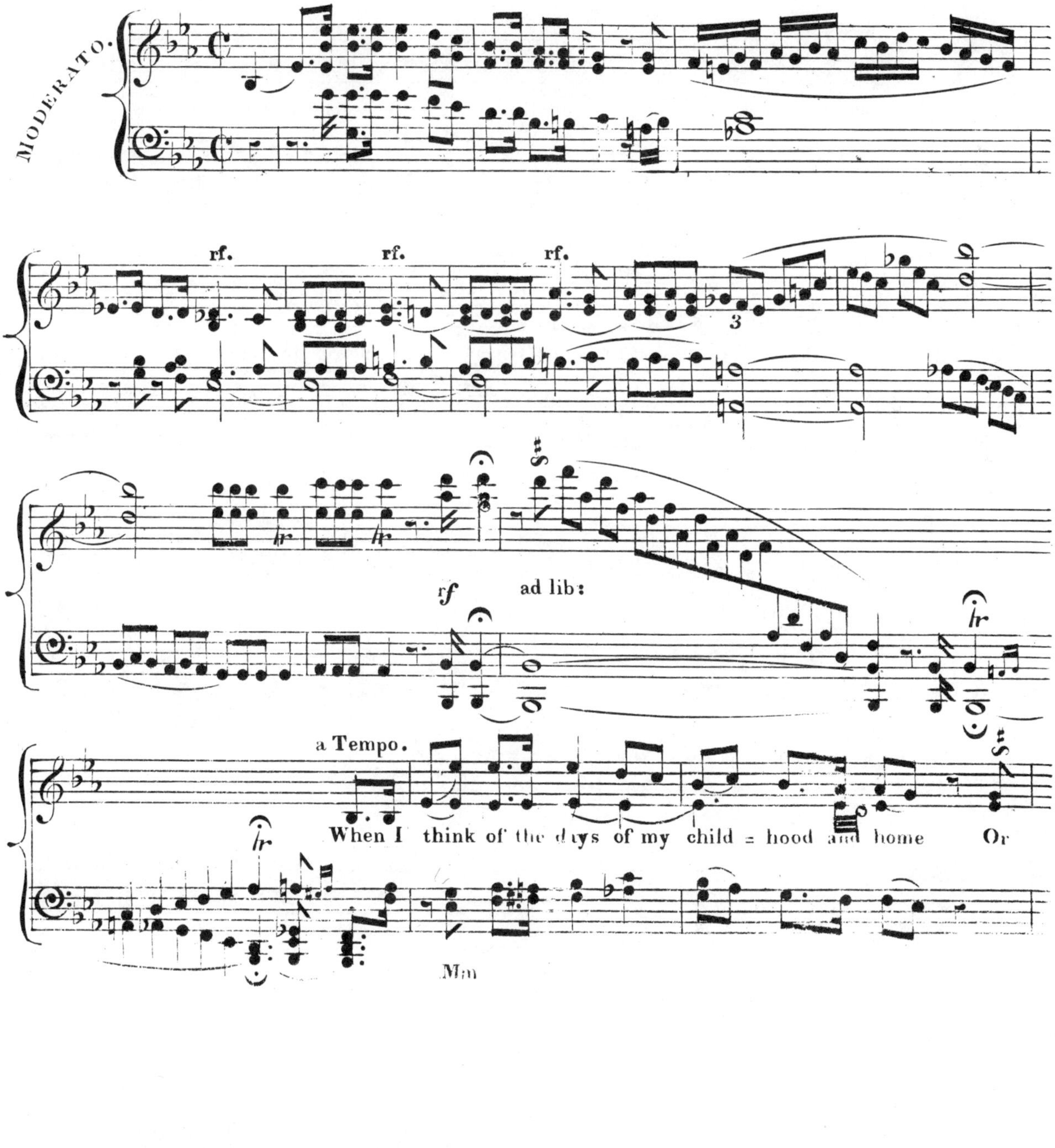

MODERATO.

rf. rf. rf.

3

tr tr

rf ad lib:

tr

a Tempo.

tr

When I think of the days of my child = hood and home Or

Mm

dream of the
that have long past a = way. The
of my heart will too
of = ten a = rise, And dar = ken the sun of the hap = piest day. Tho' thy
mountains Co = lum = bia are dear to my soul, Thy woods and thy riv = = ers sur =
pass = ingly grand, Tho' thy daughters and friends are so charm ing and true, Yet my
heart will still feel for my own native land. dol:
3

2

And I love thee, Columbia, with patriot zeal,
Thy soil ever dear. with my blood I'd defend,
Should a foe to thy freedom dare step on thy shore,
That shore, which is always the Emigrant's friend!
Then blame not the sigh that will sometimes arise,
For the land of my birth as a thought lingers there;
Yet no clime but my own, would induce me to roam,
From a country so free, and from daughters so fair!

The Poetry obligingly furnished by MR. HENRY C. LEWIS.

THE HENRIADE, A COTILLION BY A. P. HEINRICH.

(INTENDED FOR A FULL ORCHESTRA) COMPOSED AND DEDICATED

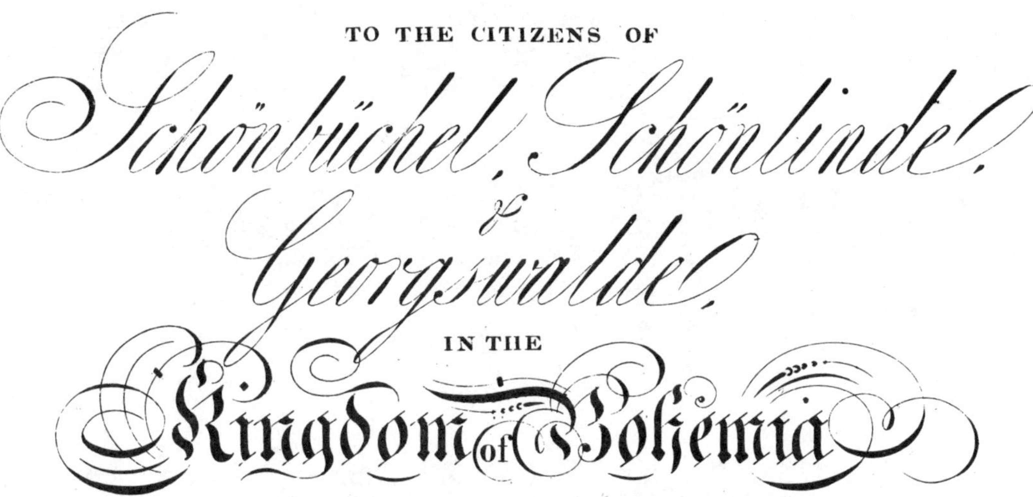

BY THEIR ABSENT COUNTRYMAN

A. P. HEINRICH.

The Author informs the American Public, that the above places, (celebrated for their flourishing Manufactories,) were the scenes of his juvenile Attachments. At Schönbüchel he entered the Gamut of Life; and at Schönlinde and Georgswalde, (places which contain more than one hundred scientific musical performers,) commenced his Chromatic Variations, in the Counterpoint of human affairs. —

Pr: 1 75.

PHILADELPHIA PUBLISHED BY BACON & HART, AND BY
THE AUTHOR, KENTUCKY.

Oo

MARCIA CONCERTANTE.

8va
loco:
Fifes.
ff Drums.
Drums.
**** Sonate o oltrapassate le misure marcate.

p
ff
p
Fine
Bugles.
TRIO.
Grazioso.

tr
tr
f
Marcia da Capo,
poi si serve del "Quickstep".
RONDO QUICK STEP.
POCO PRESTO.
espress:
3

8 va
loco.

ff
Tocca subito il Coda.

CODA — IN REMEMBRANCE OF THE MANY VIRTUES OF THE REIGNING PRINCE KINSKY, LORD OF KAMNITZ, SCHÖNLINDE, SCHÖNBÜCHEL, &C. &C.

si continua subito.

A CHEER! — IN HONOUR OF THE ILLUSTRIOUS COUNT HARRACH, LORD OF SCHLUCKENAU, GEORGSWALDE &c. &c.

8va
loco.
tr
si continua non interotto.

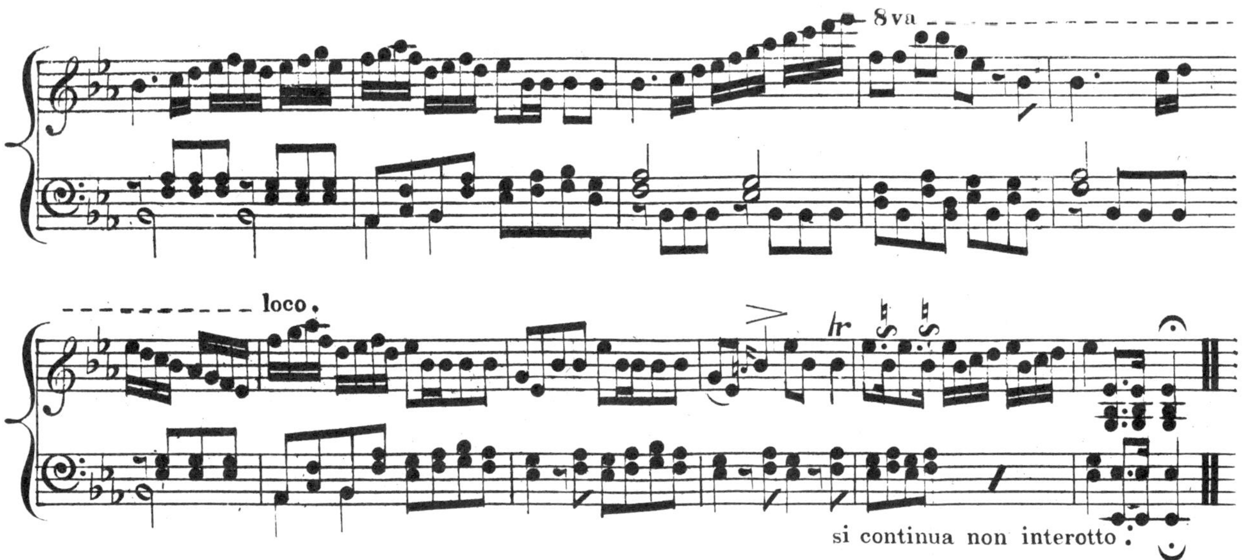

A LOYAL OBEISANCE TO HIS IMPERIAL MAJESTY, FRANCIS, II.

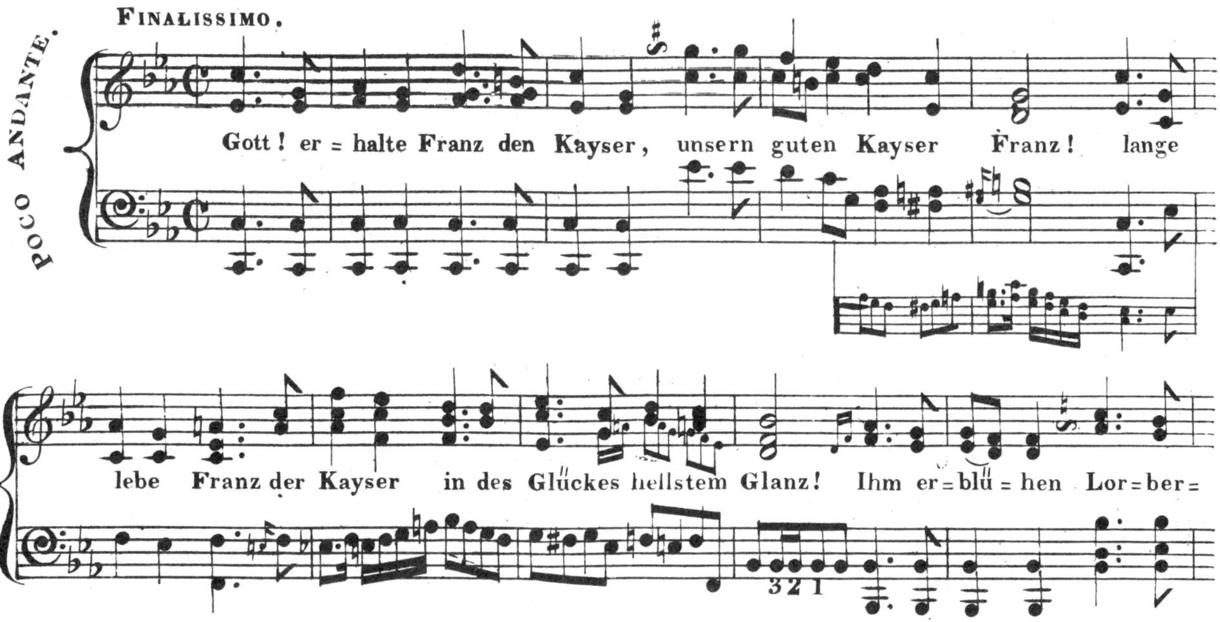
FINALISSIMO.
POCO ANDANTE.
Gott! er = halte Franz den Kayser, unsern guten Kayser Franz! lange
lebe Franz der Kayser in des Glückes hellstem Glanz! Ihm er = blü = hen Lor = ber =
321
rei = ser, wo Er geht zum Ehren = kranz! Gott! er = halte Franz der Kayser, unsern
321

gu = ten Kayser Franz. Gott! er = halte Franz den Kayser unsern gu = ten Kayser

Franz in des Glückes hellsten Glanz! Ihm er = blühen Lorber = rei = ser, wo Er

geht _ _ _ _ _ _ _ _ _ _ _ _ _ zum Eh = ren = kranz! Gott! er = halte unsern gu = ten

Kayser Franz!

8va _ _ _ _ _ _ loco. PRESTISSIMO.

ad Libitum.

tr
rf
sf
con Lic:
Bis
8va
loco
8 va

loco.
8 va
loco.
tr

8va.
loco
ff
rf.
Oc

Veloce.
rf
pp
f
p
Fine.
Oo

PIANO-FORTE;

Humbly Presented to Her Majesty
Charlotte Augusta,

EMPRESS of AUSTRIA,

By A.P. Heinrich.

PHILADELPHIA

Published by Bacon & Hart, and by the Author, Kentucky.

Price $ 3.

To her Imperial Majesty, Charlotte Auguste of Austria.

With trembling do I address your Majesty, and present you a few blossoms of my Sylvan Muse, from the American Woods. I am a native of Bohemia, a Son of misfortune, cast amid the distant regions of Kentucky. - A Babe — my child - a motherless infant - claims me back to my native soil; but alas! I apprehend, I shall never be enabled to revisit the shores of Austria, or again behold my daughter Antonia.* She was presented to me by an American Lady of superior personal and mental endowments, while on a Tour to Bohemia. A most cruel fate parted Mother and Father from the dear pledge of affection, when she had scarcely entered on this vale of tears. The tender mother rests in the silent grave - and the surviving parent, far from his native home, and that object, which alone binds him to this world, is a prey to the corrosions of sorrow and anguish.

With the patriotism and energy of a Bohemian, I can confidently assert and incontestably prove, that in a commercial point of view, I have conferred superior benefits on Austria, since my residence in the United States. During my mercantile transactions I have lost nearly a Million of Florins, and have yet considerable claims in litigation, in the Imperial Dominions, which, most probably, I shall never recover; but the sacrifice of millions would be cheerfully made, for the happiness of again pressing to my paternal bosom my child, or again to restore her the irremediable loss of a mother.

Your Majesty will vouchsafe to pardon this brief sketch of sufferings, wrested from a convulsed heart; and will sympathise with an orphan child, if not with an unfortunate father. You are the august Mother of the land — the legitimate protectress of orphans, and the widow's stay. Various reasons demand from me an explanation to the community, especially to that of my native country. I make therefore this public appeal to your Majesty, and present my helpless Infant to your throne of grace and benevolence, with the anxious hope that you will extend towards her your countenance and patronage. Fortuitously, you may foster one, whose life may be spared to prove her gratitude to her Sovereign and a blessing to Bohemia.

The Spirit of her sainted mother will watch your slumbers, and Heaven will reward the benevolence which relieves from a weight of misery, a Parent, who fervently, from the western hemisphere, offers up his orisons to the King of kings for the welfare of your Imperial family, and who, with a throbbing heart, subscribes himself an afflicted Father,

And your Majesty's most humble,
Devoted and obedient Servant,

Anthony Philip Heinrich.

Farmington, near Louisville,
Kentucky. August, 1820.

* This hapless Infant was committed to the care of a relative - an indigent but philanthropic man — Joseph Hladeck, residing on the domains of Prince Lichtenstein, at Grund, near Rumburg, — Anno Domini, one thousand, eight hundred, and fourteen.

GOD SAVE THE EMPEROR!

Crescendo e accelerando:
a Tempo.
f
p
tr
con Licenza.
espress:
tr
dol:
rf
legato.
10
tr
tr
Pp

cres - - - - - cen - - - - - - - - - - - do.
rf
ritardando:
rf
POCO ALLEGRO.
VAR:
2.
Pr

sf
sf
VAR:
3.

8va
loco:
8va
*
w
VAR:
4.
3
Pp
* Optional.

8va.
loco:
8va.
loco:
alla Cadenza
tr
Pp

tr
ritard:
VAR:
5.
tr
tr
tr
8
6
3
Pp

8 va.
loco.
CODA.
10
6
12
12
Segue gli Minuetti.
Pp

FIVE MINUETS.

THE IMPERIAL.

* The following Minuets are more especially intended for the Violin.

Min: D.C.
THE ROYAL.
MINUET.
Fin:
TRIO.

D.C.
321
8
THE ILLUSTRIOUS.
MINUET.
321
TRIO.

THE AFFABLE.
MINUET.
TRIO.
l'Accompagnamento pizzicato
La prima volta senza l'Appogiature.
l'Arco.

Minuetto D.C.
THE PHILANTHROPIC.
MINUET.
TRIO.
Pp

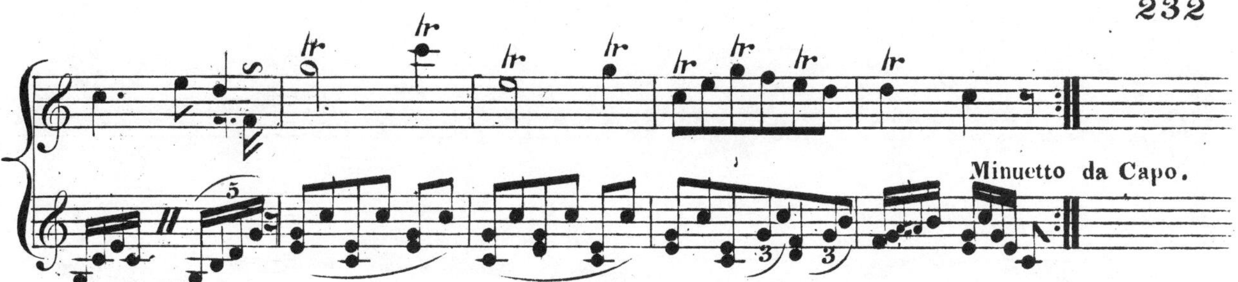

Note _ The principal traits of the foregoing Trio, I have adapted, from memory, in honour of the Manes of their Author, a schoolmate of mine, Mr. Anthony Friedrich, (a native of Schoenlinde,) who was cut off in his youth; and though his fame probably never passed beyond the Village Chronicles, yet was he one of the finest geniusses, that nature ever produced; and even in his juvenile years, a great performer on all the principal Instruments of the Orchestra.

A. P. H.

THE AUSTRIAN _ A LANDLER.

Pp

Pp

8 va
loco:
Pp

3
5

rf
321
Pp

Segue "The Fair Traveller."
Fine.

KRÁSNÁ POCESTNÁ.

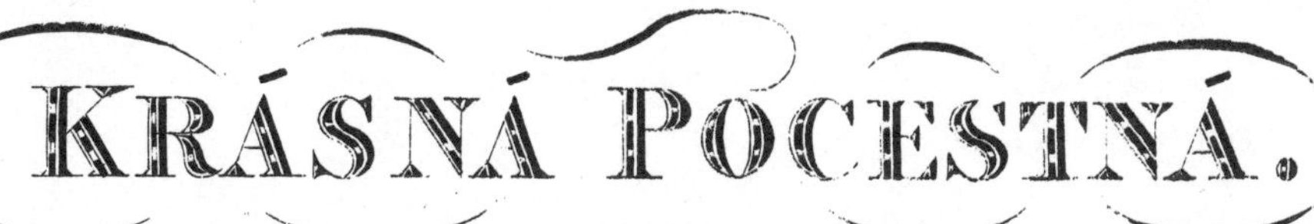

A NEB

Gizda Postečný z Prahý do Widně

(WIHLASSENY WALZER.)

THE FAIR TRAVELLER.

or the

POST-RIDE FROM PRAGUE TO VIENNA.

A DESCRIPTIVE WALTZ.

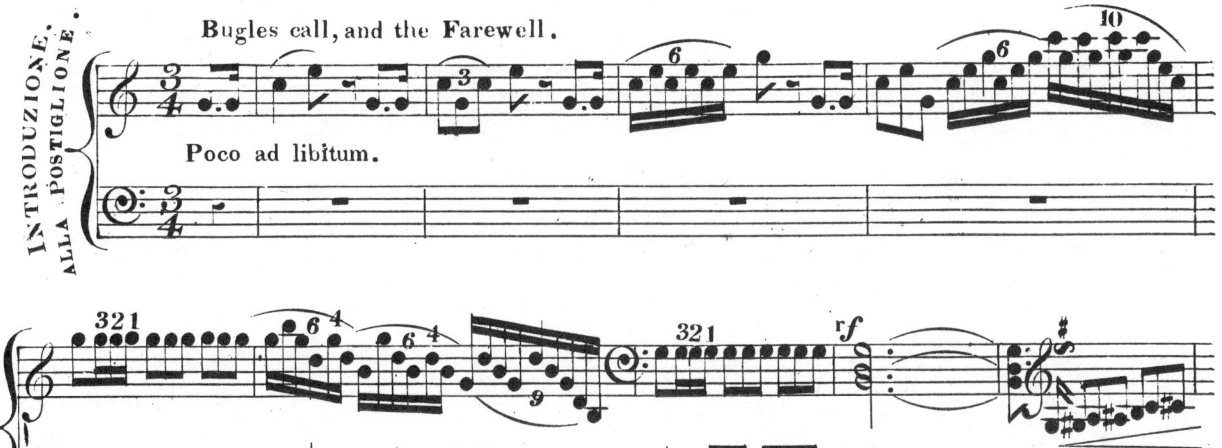
INTRODUZIONE.
ALLA POSTIGLIONE.
Bugles call, and the Farewell.
Poco ad libitum.
ritard:

THE DEPARTURE.

* The following Airs are principally calculated for the Violin, as the most imitative Instrument of the Bugle or Post Horn.

BÖHMISCHBROD. (Corda G sopra il Violino.)
loco
IGLAU. (sul D o il G e D.)

Moravian Mountains.
sul D e A.
Whipping the Horses.
3 2 1
ZNAIM. (sul G.)
3 2 1
The inspiring Whip again.
8va
Vine Hills of Austria.
Pp

loco.
Spurring.
Kicking.
(sopra il G.)
STOCKERAU and the DANUBE.
Legato.

1st
2d
ENZERSDORF.
in full speed.
HAIL VIENNA!

Zastaw w Cÿsarownè z Rakaus.*
Empress's March.
GIUSTO.
* Stop at the Empress of Austria.
Pp

6
5
9
6
8va
loco:
cres:
3 2 1
3 2 1
Pp

8va
tr
6
loco.
3
8 va.
loco.
rf
con o senza Trillo.
Pp

6
6
3
3
5
5
7
321
32
1
321
321
6
2da volta
Pp

2da
8 va
loco
alla Trio:

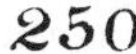

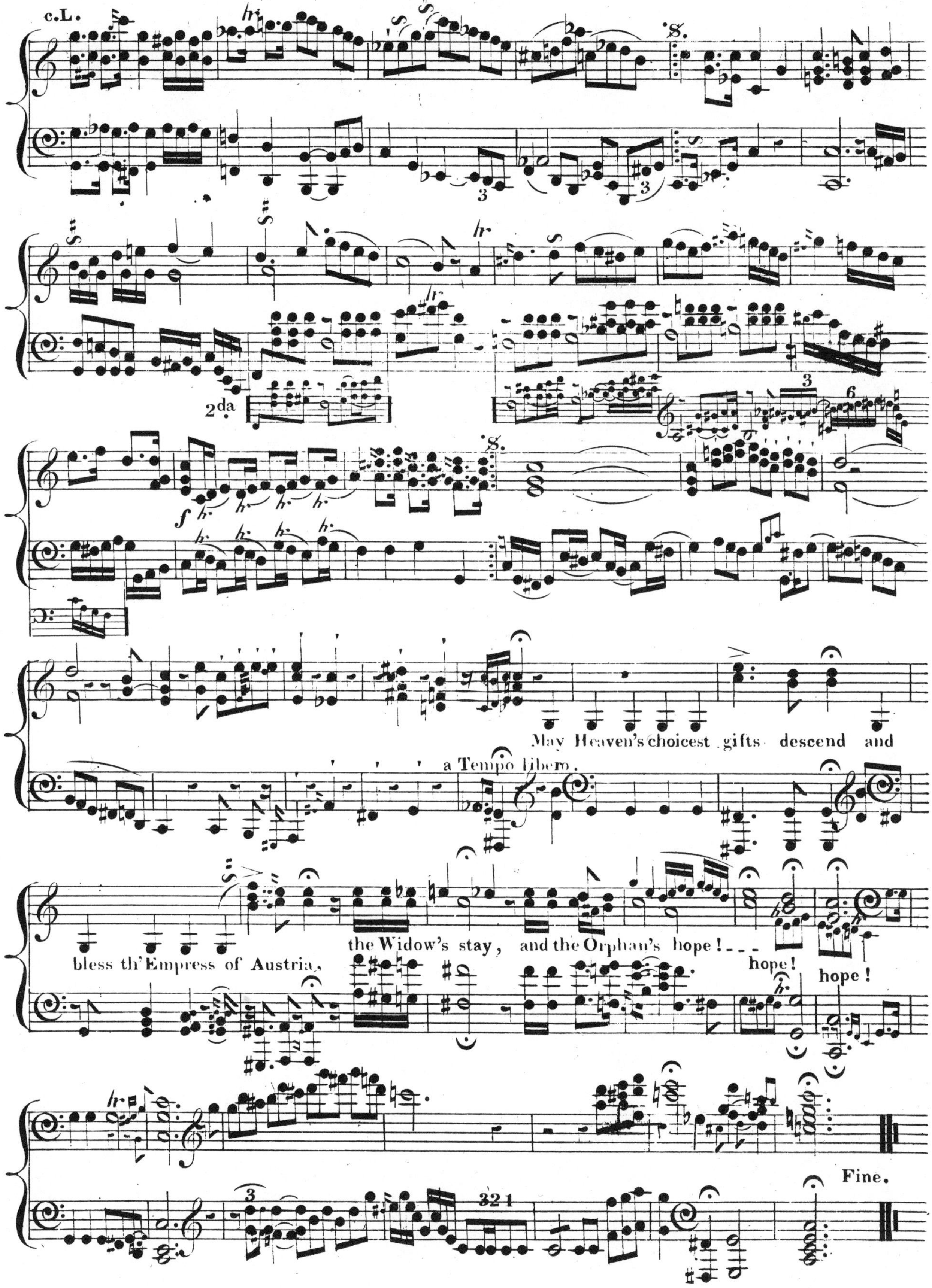

c.L.

2da

a Tempo libero.

May Heaven's choicest gifts descend and bless th'Empress of Austria, the Widow's stay, and the Orphan's hope! - - - hope! hope!

Fine.

DIVERTIMENTO,

DEDICATED TO THE VERY LIBERAL

Patrons of the Science

IN THE

UNITED STATES,

AS A VERY SMALL

Mite of Gratitude

FROM

A. P. HEINRICH.

 Gratis.

PHILADELPHIA, PUBLISHED BY BACON & HART, AND
BY THE AUTHOR, KENTUCKY.

ENTRATA.

ALLA TROMBETTA.
VIOLINO PRINCIPALE.
VIOLINO 1mo.
VIOLINO 2do.
BASSO O VIOLONCELLO.
PIANO FORTE.
8va
CADENZA.
loco.
V. S.
con Libertà!

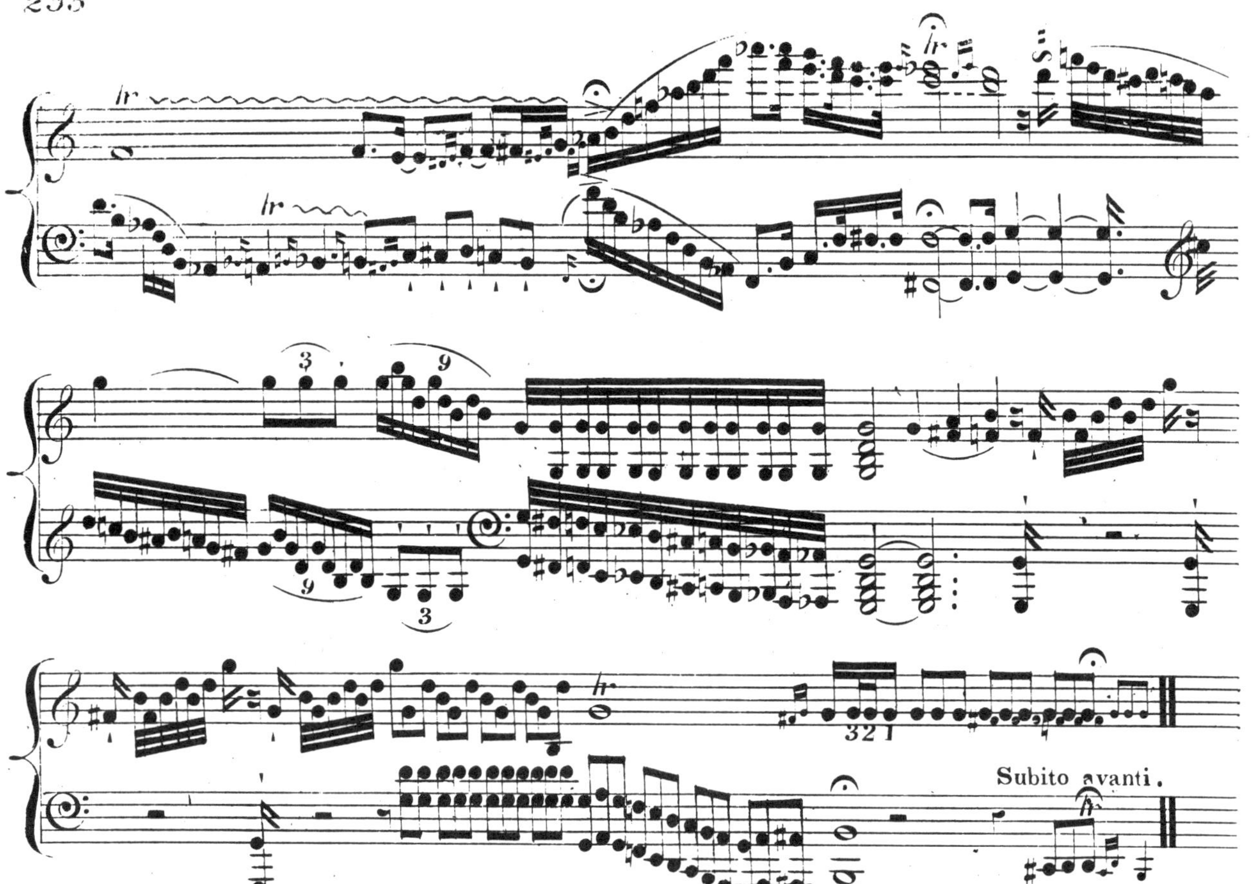

N.B. Whether the following modifications, (Pizzicato, con Sordini, &c. &c.) are calculated either in whole or in part, to produce an agreeable contrast, the Author could not practically ascertain; it is therefore left to the judgment of the Performers.

loco.
D
A D
A
8 va.

loco.

alla Cadenza (con Egualità!)
Poco piu Presto.
Sordino e arcato.
Sordino e arcato.
senza Sordino, pizzicato.
con Sordino e L'arco.
6
senza sordino Pizzicato.
8va
tremolante.

Ad Lib:
Sordino L'arco.
loco
Tacet.
Violino principale.
Yankee Doodle.
Tempo Allegretto.
Senza gli sordini.

NOTE — Accompany the following Variations with the foregoing Theme,(sempre da Capo con Precisione.) After Variations No. 9. and 14. strike up Yankee Doodlé, quasi Prestissimo alla Crowdero.

VARIATIONS.

* The Interlineations, will, whilst they add variety, improve the corresponding Harmony.

VAR: 6.
VAR: 7.
VAR: 8.
VAR: 9.
un Arco Solo.

at one Bow.
Take breath good Signor, pray dismiss these quakes,
Such Doodleiads, I know, have dreadful shakes,
But "breast thee to the shock", yet rest awhile,
And let this Band in truest Yankee style
And jiggling cant, these yawners now beguile
Of half their dreams. —
INTERLUDIO, POCO GRAVE. (subito dopo Yankeedoodle)
VIOLINO PRINCIPALE.
Con Sordini e delicato.
VIOLONCELLO.
Violino 1mo, 2do e Piano Forte, Tacet.
pizzicato.
arcato.
a Piacere.
levate gli Sordini.
Pizz:
Arco
Yankee Doodle — what a shake !!!
Sure such a shake's the dandy,
A shake of shakes, a mighty shake!
O shake it! shake it handy !!!!
VIOLONCELLO TACET.
YANKEE DOODLE SHAKE.
sempre legato

HUZZA FOR WASHINGTON!
VIOLINO PRINCIPALE
Alla Marcia, Allegramente.
VIOLONCELLO.
Pizzicato.
L'arco.
ff
c:L:
Volti Subito.

Poco Lentemente.
Piu presto quasi alla Cadenza.
accelerando.
sf
Continuate subito.
Da qui il Violino 1mo 2do e Basso sempre pizzicato.
Var 10
rf
Tempo di Tema.
8va

Var: 11.
Var: 12.
Var: 13.
8va
loco.

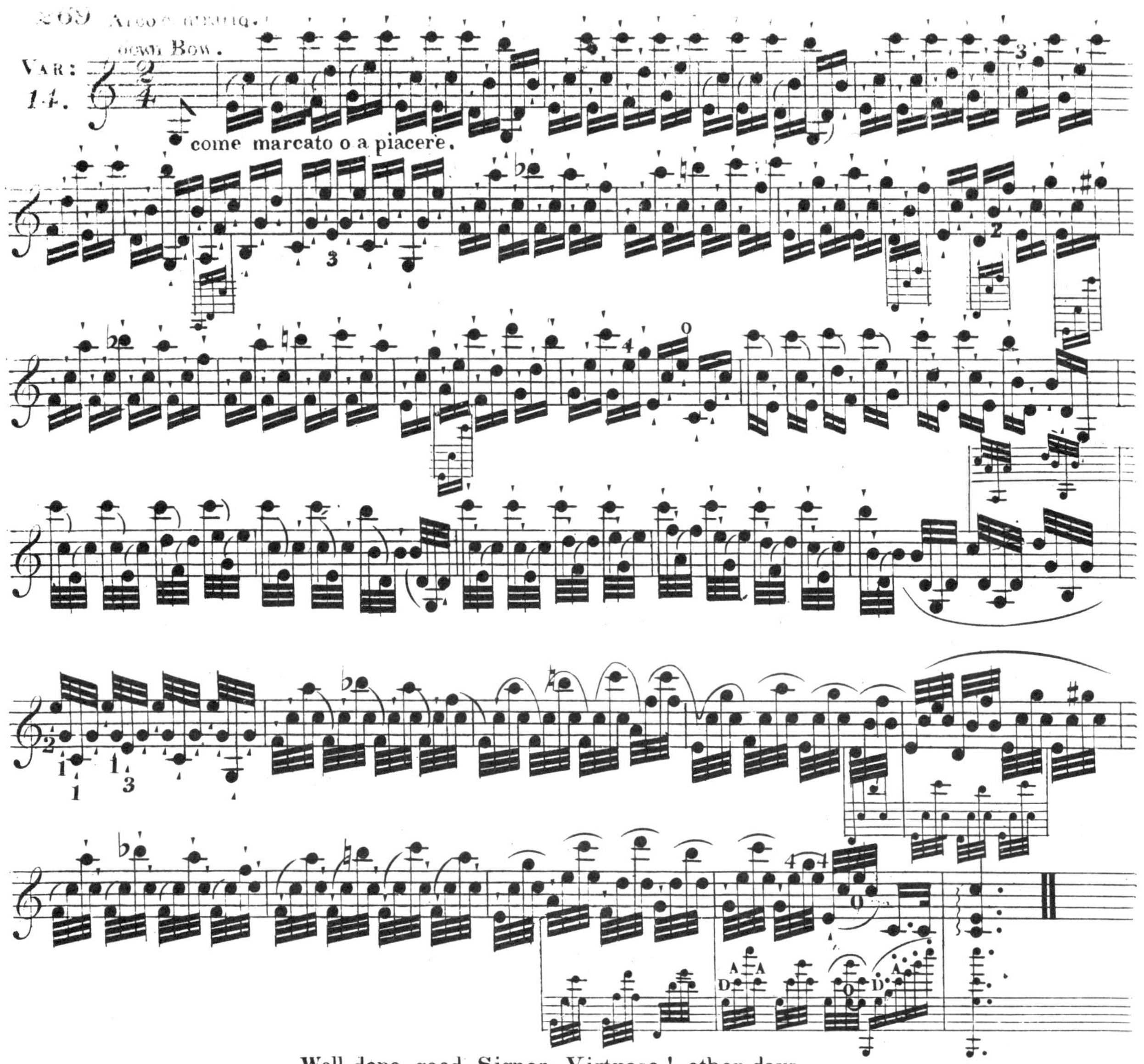

Well done good Signor Virtuoso! other days,
When rest does calm thy ague fit, shall blaze
Thy matchless deeds — up thy Cremona hang;
Let no rude Yankee Doodleiad, e'er twang
Again its cords, or shake thee with such pain
To pay a MITE, or LIBERAL PATRONS gain.

Now take your stand, ye mighty Band,
With Fiddle, Drum, and Trumpet,
Da Capo Yankee Doodle doo,
As loud as ye can thump it.

Join all the glee — All colours free*
From reckonings, duns, and gripers;
MARCH! beat the flam, for Uncle Sam‖
Pays all, but SCRIBES and Pipers.

*"Gratis", see title page.

‖Eldest son of Old YANKEE DOODLE.

THE WESTERN MINSTREL

‘Neque semper arcum tendit Apollo.’

A. P. HEINRICH presents this Supplement to the First Volume of the "Dawning of Music in Kentucky," and, although he could have wished to enrich it with a greater variety of Musical Subjects, expressly composed for, and peculiarly adapted to, the nature of its character, yet, his inability to sustain the unexpected expences of the publication has obliged him, reluctantly, to yield to circumstances, and leave the meditated Plan of the Work, in a partial degree, undeveloped, although sixty pages have been furnished more than originally contemplated in the Prospectus.

This addition, though attended with accumulated pecuniary embarrassment, has been cheerfully made, with the fervent hope, that the "Dawning of Music" may approach nearer the Meridian of Light; but, whether the clouds, which yet darken the horizon, will ever be completely dispelled, the Author leaves to Time, the genial Influence of the Muse, and the Sympathy of the Public, to determine.

Notwithstanding his most strenuous exertions, A. P. HEINRICH, *very sensibly*, experiences, that the Profession to which he is most enthusiastically attached, and to which all his energies have been devoted, will not, for want of more general patronage and support, afford him even a *bare subsistence*:† but, while bowing to the public ordeal, he cannot avoid, on the present occasion, cherishing the expectation of that support to which he is entitled, in order to fulfil the numerous obligations incurred in this experimental publication.

To attain this desirable object, those noble spirited friends who patronized the undertaking in *Kentucky*, and who, almost exclusively, deigned to interest themselves for the SYLVAN MINSTREL, are respectfully solicited to comply with their engagements. By acceding to this request, they will not only reflect some genial *rays of sunshine* on the "Dawning of Music" in their *native* State, but also erect for themselves an honourable monument, as Patrons of a Work which (should it possess no other merit) claims public attention, at all events, as being a truly original effort of the Art....and primitive in Regions, particularly, where, since the yell of the war-whoop has become *tacet*......the whistling of the tomahawk and other *Furiosos* of the ruthless savage ceased to vibrate, scarcely any other strains are heard than the *music of the axe, the hammer's din, or the cadences of the Banjo.*

The Author laments that he cannot also wield the above-mentioned instruments, as they are so much more generally understood, and beyond comparison *more profitable*. This regret is elicited, from the true cause.....that he finds himself so scantily supported in his pursuits of Melody and Harmony, as almost to make it appear that Plutus was at mortal variance with Apollo, and that the Muses, on account of the strife, would be obliged to quit the field, or, at best, to hang their harps unstrung on the willow. A hope, however, is still entertained, that Plutus, with his *tinkling golden* sounds, and the *Prima Vistas* of *Notes alla Banco*, has not so entirely enslaved the Public, as to induce them to turn a deaf ear to the *Tones*, or protest the *Notes* of the *poor* Sons of Orpheus. A. P. Heinrich sincerely wishes this, for the prosperity of the Sublime Art, and the respect due to his Musical Brethren; as, for himself, he solely trusts, that, *if* Music refines Mankind, improves the heart, and evinces a superior degree of civilization, the Minstrel of Kentucky will not be considered altogether a *blank* in Society.

He cannot however, refrain, on this occasion, from candidly mentioning, that, during his short Musical Career, the most humble applications for patronage have been made to persons in *high life;* but, instead of receiving fostering smiles of encouragement, or even the Melodies of friendly answers, he has too often found, that

> Some men there are, cold as the Winter's snow,
> Whose souls ne'er felt bland Music's sacred glow.....

A glow of mental pleasure is, however, derived from having this opportunity of expressing his heartfelt gratitude to Mess'rs Joshua Fry, John Speed, Willis Lee, Isaac Thom, Peter Grayson, James Black, Henry Maltz, and I. C. Wenzel, of Kentucky; also, to Mr. Charles Voltz, of Pittsburg, who voluntarily exerted themselves to obtain subscriptions for the Publication, and, in other respects, testified their friendship for the Author.

Agreeably to the engagement in the Prospectus, a printed List of Subscribers should be furnished; but, although every exertion has been made to obtain the names of the liberal *few* who have assisted the Dawning of Music with some vivifying rays of philanthropy, yet the Author's efforts have been hitherto unavailing. The Nomenclature, will, he trusts, be published at a more fortuitous period.

That every blessing may attend the Friends and Sons of the Muses......that the Arts and Sciences may flourish in the New World, and, that the *utile dulce* may be duly appreciated, in every liberal profession, is the sincere desire of

the Public's humble servant,

A. P. HEINRICH, of Kentucky.

† The above will be readily believed, when it is stated, that, only a few days ago, Dame *Capriccio* so frowned on the ill-fated Author, as to *transpose* him *sforzando*, to the diatonic, chromatic, en-harmonic, *Turnkey* of one of those hospitable public mansions, where the unfortunate finds an Asylum, *free* and *safe*; Bread and Water to prolong starvation, and a Brick, cold as the heart of the extortionate, for a Pillow, however trifling the demand, he may be called upon by a creditor *alla falsetto o rubato.*

PHILADELPHIA, 1820.

PHILADELPHIA, PUBLISHED FOR THE AUTHOR, BY BACON &CO.

MUSIC SELLERS, 11. SOUTH FOURTH STREET.

HAST THOU SEEN!

FROM "SONGS OF JUDAH," BY W. B. TAPPAN.

Canto D.C.

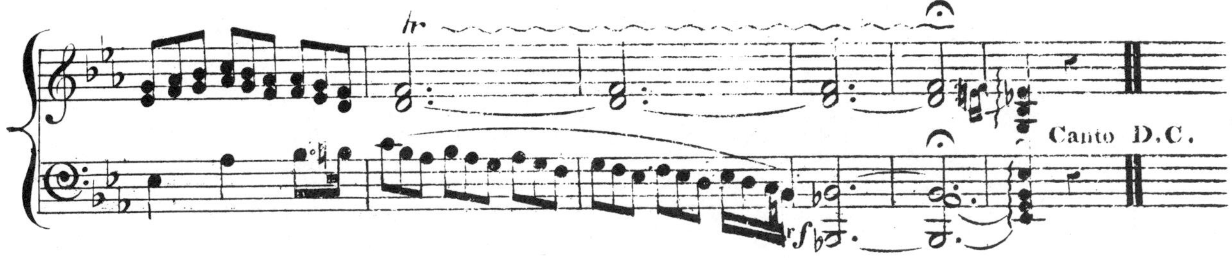

2

Hast thou seen — the tempest over —
Radiant suns again illume;
Threatening storms no longer hover,
Nature bud with fresher bloom?
Thus, through darkest clouds of even,
Smiles the opening dawn of heaven!

PHILADELPHIA WALTZ. An extract from the "Visit to Philadelphia."

SOAVE

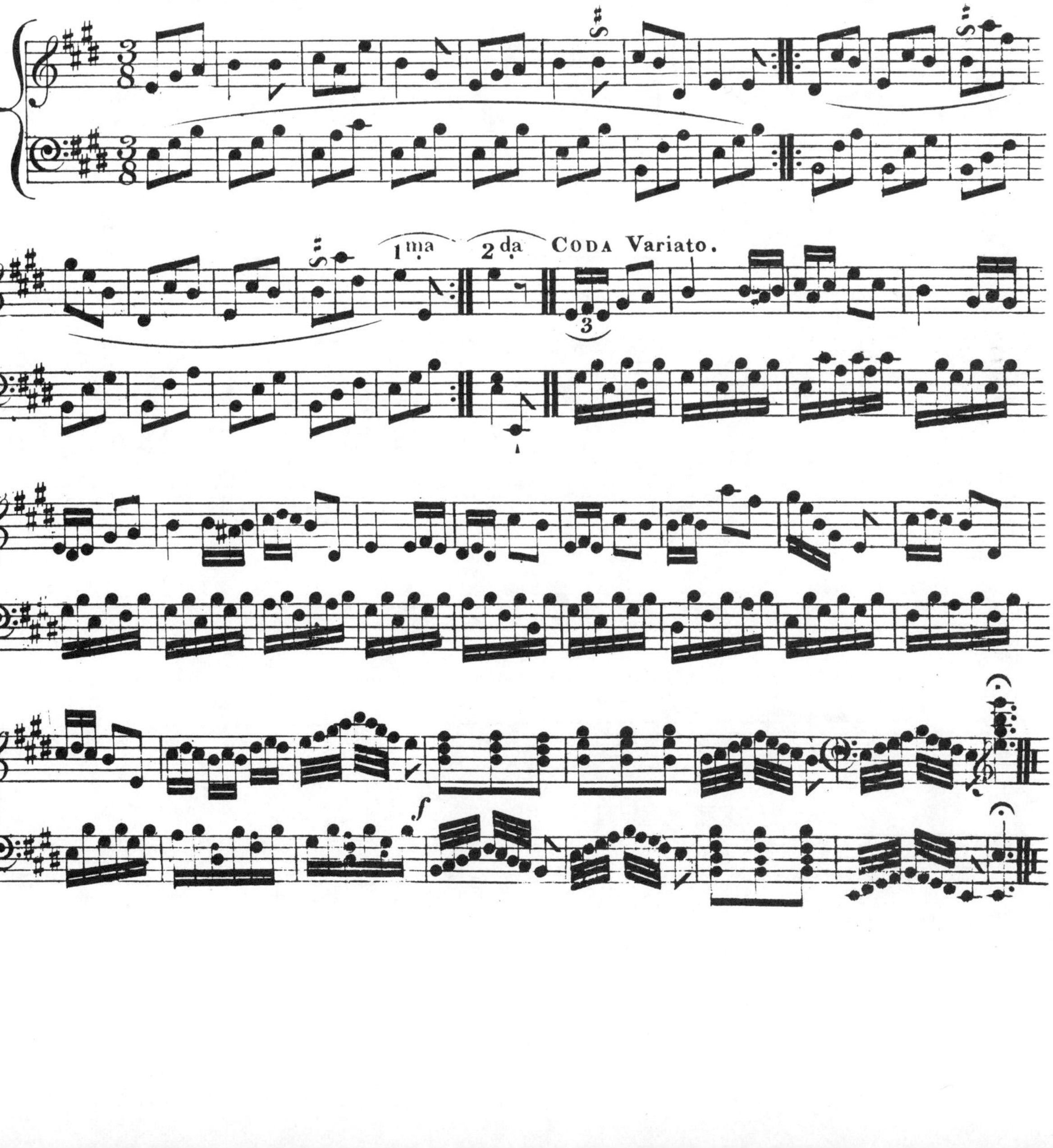
1ma
2da
CODA Variato.

REMEMBER ME!

POETRY BY H. C. LEWIS.

AS SUNG by Miss C. Mc MANUSS.

Poco Allegretto.

Dol: espress: dol: fin. p

Re=member me while the heart can beat, Re=member me while the rose is sweet, While the rose is sweet on its hum=ble tree To feel=ing souls, re=mem=ber me. remem=ber me!

Minore. dol:

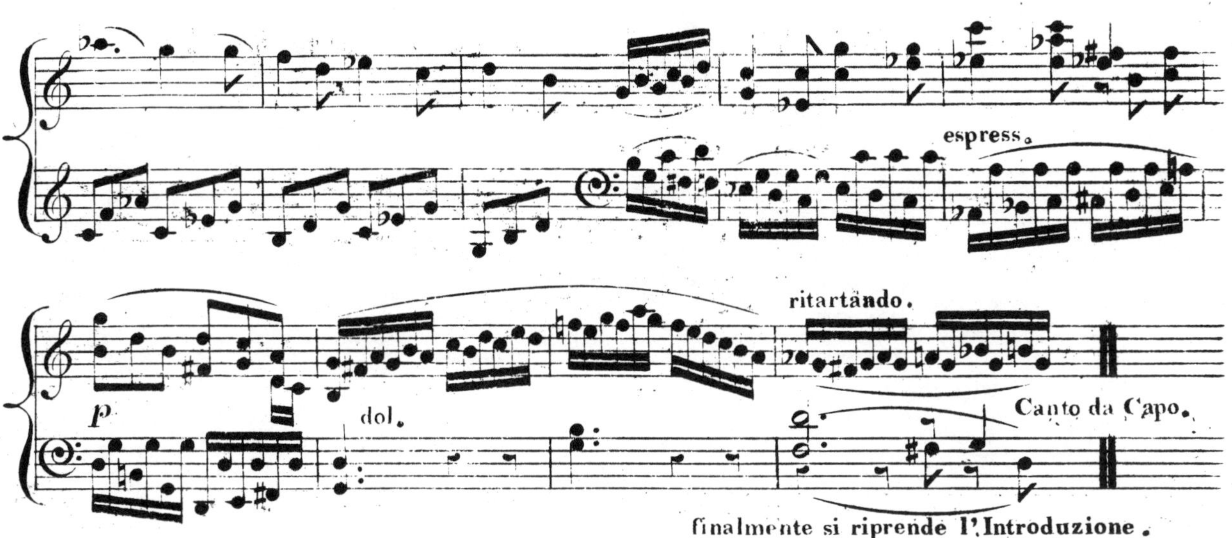

2
Remember me, while a nerve can feel
The thorns which spring from a heart of steel
While a heart of steel is a thorny tree
Without a flow'r, remember me!

3
Remember me, while the smile of eyes
Can raise the soul to the bliss of skies:
While the bliss of skies, to misery
Is turn'd by frowns, remember me!

4
Remember me, while the willow weeps,
In night dew tears, where the lover sleeps:
While the willow weeps, for his agony,
Around his grave, remember me!

The Yager's Adieu!
ALLA CACCIA.
MOLTO ANIMATO.
On prancing steeds three Ya = gers sprang, A = dieu, Adieu, A = dieu! Their sweethearts fair thus sweet = ly sang, A = dieu, Adieu, A = dieu! No other tear shall stain, they cried, The cheek a warriors kiss has dried, A = dieu, Adieu, A = dieu, Adieu! Then all for glo = ry fly! Then
sempre crescendo.
Copy right secured

2

A thousand more are on the field,
Adieu, &c.
With martial sounds the skies are fill'd,
Adieu, &c.
Then where is he so mean and shy,
In woman's arms would trembling lie,
Adieu, &c.
When all for glory fly!
Huzza! &c.

3

And where, young warrior dost thou fly?
Adieu, &c
With dauntless brow and eagle eye,
Adieu, &c
To meet the foe that fiercely comes,
To spoil our fields and sacred homes,
Adieu, &c
I too for glory fly!
Huzza! &c

4

Our Country calls — the Yager hears,
Adieu, &c.
We give her hope, and calm her fears,
Adieu, &c.
Then for the foe — and leave behind,
On its bleak sides the mountain wind,
Adieu, &c.
When we for glory fly!
Huzza! &c

5

Where cannons dread their lightnings flash,
Adieu, &c.
And sword meets sword in fearful crash,
Adieu, &c.
The Yager there still spurs his steed,
Whilst 'neath his hoof the foe doth bleed,
Adieu, &c.
For we to glory fly!
Huzza! &c.

6

But now we pant for war's alarms,
Adieu, &c
To Love, and Beauty's twining arms
Adieu, &c
We go — but in the dreadful fight,
For us, dark dangers path you'll light,
Adieu, &c
For all to glory fly!
Huzza! &c

Note — At the request of many of his friends, the Author publishes this Song in its present form: He regrets that the limits of the present Work, would not allow the Original Embellishments, and the German Poetry; for which he refers to "The Dawning of Music" — The foregoing translation is from the pen of his esteemed friend, P. Grayson Esq. of Bardstown, Ky.

Maid of the Valley.

WRITTEN BY W. B. TAPPAN.

2

I am thine only,
O how sincerely!
True to thee, dearest, will I remain;
When far away,
A stranger I wander,
Thoughts of my charmer will glad me again!

VENEZ ICI!

WORDS BY H. C. LEWIS, PHILAD.

ALLEGRAMENTE SCHERZANDO.

Venez ici! Venez ici! Venez ici! my dearest care, And

Sospirando.
bless me with thy warmest smile, And bless me with thy
warm = est smile; Return but love for love, my fair, And life is joy, midst
every toil! Venez ici! Venez ici! Venez!
Venez ici! (yes) (si! si! si! si si!)

2

Venez ici!
Venez ici!
Venez ici! Be not so coy —
Fear not — I could not do thee harm!
Trust me, my love, thy every joy
I'll guard as safe as every charm!
Venez ici!

3

Venez ici!
Venez ici!
Venez ici! O my fond heart
Beats but for thine, for only thine!
Let them, then, throb no more apart —
O come, my Love, be only mine!
Venez ici!

The Musical Bachelor.

The same Air differently arranged, with an Accompaniment for the Flute, may be found in "The Dawning of Music." The Poetry is politely furnished by J. R. Black Esq. of Shelbyville, Ky.

I would not wed the fair = = est lass, That ev = er sway'd on
beau = = ty's throne; Un = less her heart like mir = ror'd glass, My ev' = ry feel = = ing,
pas = sion, shone.
I would not
wed the wit = = tiest maid, That ev = = = er touch'd a mor = = tal's heart =
= =, Un = less her darts were mere = ly played, In simple in = no = cen = cy's part.
p
tr
Innocente.
Canto D.C.

3

I would not wed the purest soul,
That ever feeling governed most;
Unless her heart would bear control,
And of its goodness never boast.

4

I would not wed —' all else her own,
A Queen, devoid of music's taste;
With her, my heart would be alone,
Her palace seem a dreary waste.

* A rustic Waltz.

There is an hour of peaceful rest.*

FROM "NEW ENGLAND AND OTHER POEMS", BY W. B. TAPPAN.

*AS SUNG by Miss C. Mc MANUSS.

Where are the pleasures of Life

WRITTEN BY G. DUTTON.

3

Gay riches, which all would possess,
May dazzle and charm for a while;
But when racked with pain will they bless—
On the face of disease light a smile ?

4

Blest Hygeia, that joy giving power,
May tend oft from trouble to save;
But will it from death beds insure,
Or exempt mortal man from the grave ?

5

Kind Friendship a care soothing balm,
May assuage with its tender of love;
But the terrors of death will it calm ?
Ah no! nought but peace from above.

6

Then where are the pleasures of life,
That mortals may hope to enjoy;
O where is content void of strife,
And the peace that is free from annoy ?

Irradiate Cause!

FROM "SONGS OF JUDAH" BY W. B. TAPPAN.

4

Thee we adore! but mortal praise,
How faint compared with Gabriel's song;
With thee how weak our noblest lays,
Thou Dread, to whom all Powers belong.

5

Help us, O Thou! 'tis thou alone
Canst touch our lips with living fire;
Though frail, we would approach thy throne;
Though dust, attempt an angel's lyre.

6

Accept our incense, and control
Each power, each wish, O God, to thee!
Receive the broken, contrite soul,
The offering dear to Deity!

Image of my Tears.

WRITTEN BENEATH A PICTURE BY LORD BYRON.

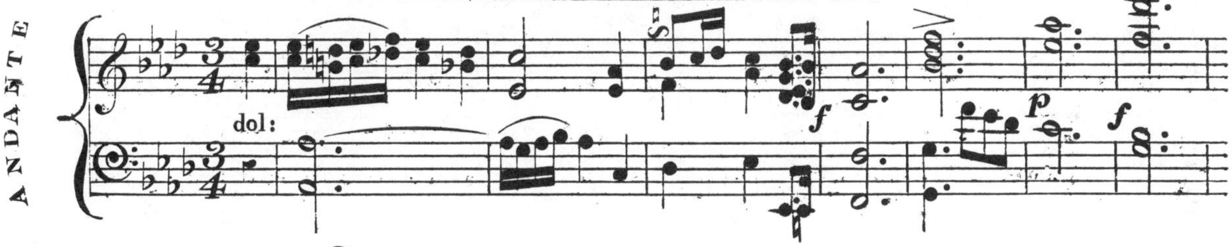

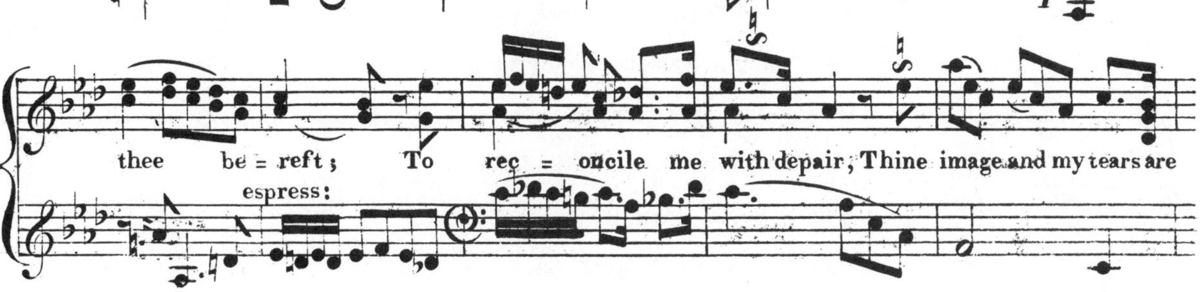

ANDANTE

dol: f p f

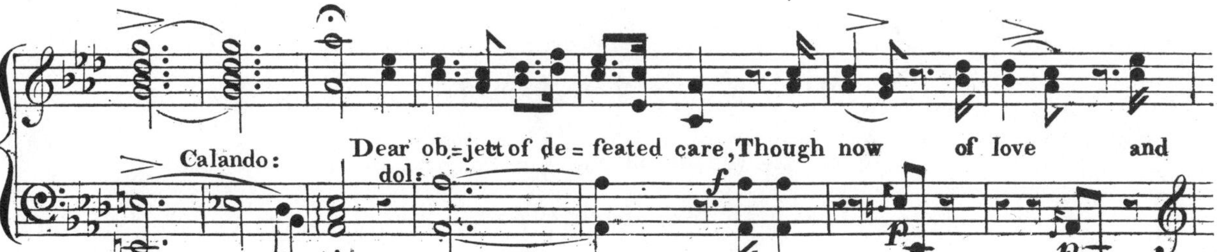

Calando: dol:

Dear ob = jett of de = feated care, Though now of love and

f p p

thee be = reft; To rec = oncile me with depair, Thine image and my tears are

espress:

2. Verse.

WRITTEN BY H.C. LEWIS.

From Heaven, in sublimest peace,
Look down, dear shade, on earthly woe,
Where sad regret can never cease
To bid my tears incessant flow:
Dear saint, look down with pitying eyes,
O! look into my heart and see,
Where, borne upon its deepest sighs,
Each anxious thought returns to thee.

GIPSEY DANCE.

2

He dreamt of his home, of his dear native bowers,
And pleasure that waited on life's merry morn;
While Memory stood sideway, half covered with (flowers,
And restored every rose, but secreted its thorn.

3

Then Fancy her magical pinions spread wide,
And bade the young dreamer in exstacy rise,
Where far, far behind him the green waters glide,
And the cot of his forefathers blesses his eyes.

4

A Father bends o'er him with looks of delight,
His cheeks are impearled with a mother's warm tear,
And the lips of the boy in a love kiss unite
With the lips of the maid whom his bosom holds (dear.

5

The heart of the sleeper beats high in his breast,
Joy quickens his pulse — all hardships seem o'er,
A thrill of bright exstacy steals o'er his rest,
"O God! thou hast blessed me — I ask for no more."

FROM "SONGS OF JUDAH" BY W. B. TAPPAN.

LENTEMENTE E INNOCENTE.

Ye kind benevo=lent, that know Of intellectual bliss the sum; Ye whose expanded feelings glow, Oh smile up= on the Deaf and Dumb! On them the storm have rudely blown, They wither on the breast of even, Re=ceive the flowrets to your own, Their fragrance shall as=cend to heaven, Their fragrance shall as=cend

3

Oh let these too, in knowledge share,
From the waste mind let darkness flee,
Bid the bright day-beam kindle there,
The lamp to immortality!

4

Though soothing blandishment ne'er cheers
Their solitude, nor utterance kind,
Yet mutual sympathy is their's,
The language of the kindred mind.

5

And this shall bless you — and the tear,
Nature's pure accent — shall reveal
Emotions undefined — yet dear,
The tribute which the heart can feel.

6

Yes! and the bosom whispered prayer
Of innocence shall rise, while some
Winged messenger, to God, shall bear
The offering of the Deaf and Dumb!

Love in Ohio.*

WRITTEN BY H. C. LEWIS.

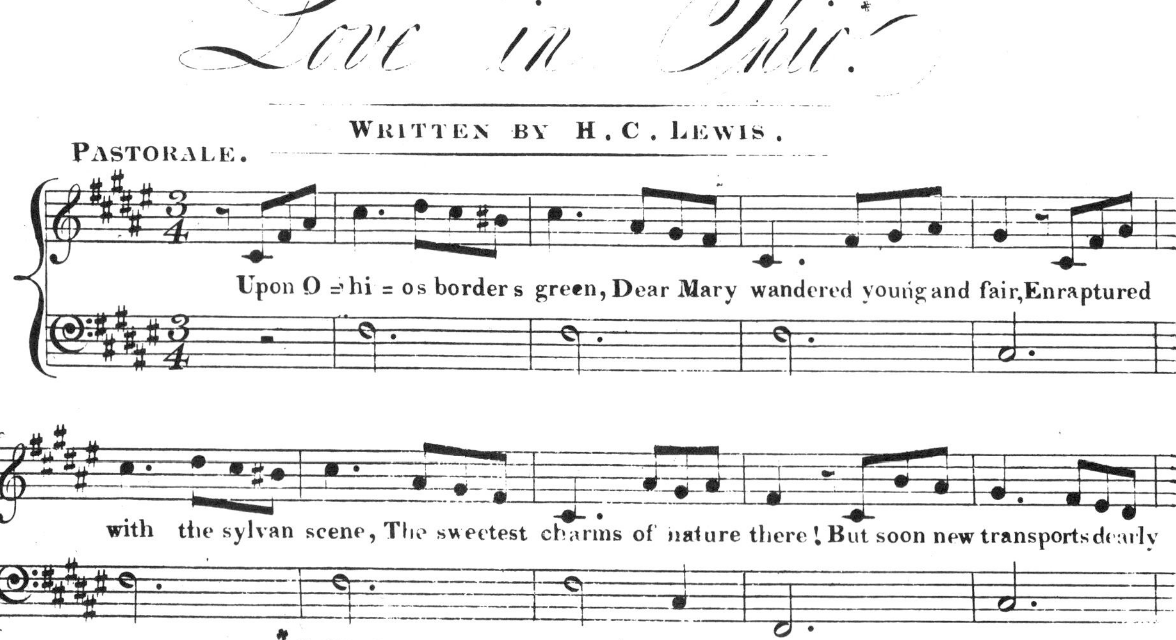

*SUNG by Miss V. BOUDET.

2

The Maiden's cheeks were crimsoned o'er,
As Edgar breathed his vows of love;
While sighs and blushes told him more,
Than language e'er attempts to prove.
They pledged their faith forever there,
And blessed the hallowed spot serene;
And now they rove the happiest pair,
Upon Ohio's borders green.

THE MINSTREL'S MARCH,

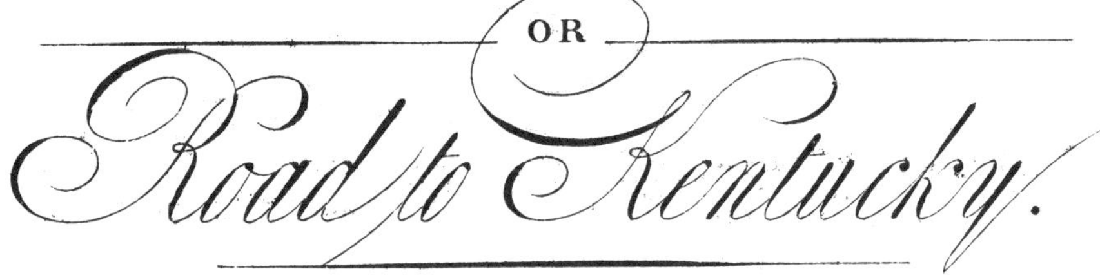

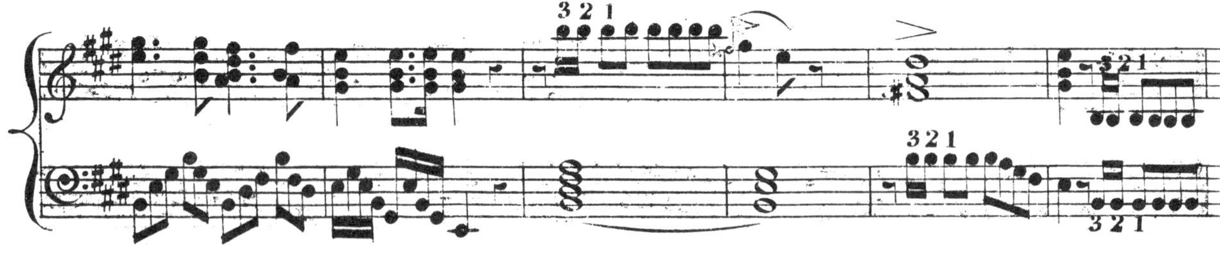

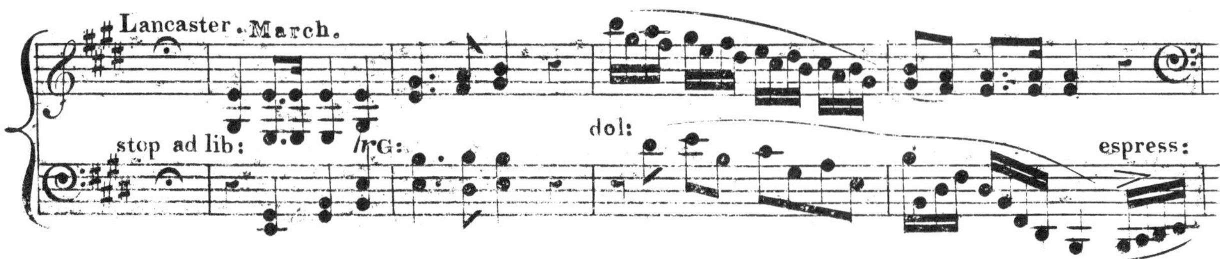

Alleghanies.
321
321
321
Fort Pitt.
rf
rf
rf
rf
Embarcation.
321
321

Salute. sempre cresendo.
rf
rf
rf
rf
rf
3 2 1
Passage on the Ohio.
dolce.
tr
The Rapids.
ff

Standing in for Port.
Casting Anchors.
sf
Landing and cheers.
3 2 1
Side steps.
rf
3 2 1
32 1
3 2 1
3 2 1
sempre crescendo.
3
3
rf
rf
rf
rf
5
5
8 va
loco.
cres
cen
do.
3 2 1
5
3 2 1
Sign of the Harp.